Solomon Cro

Solomon Crow's Christmas Pockets and Other Tales

by Ruth McEnery Stuart

His mother named him Solomon because, when he was a baby, he looked so wise; and then she called him Crow because he was so black. True, she got angry when the boys caught it up, but then it was too late. They knew more about crows than they did about Solomon, and the name suited.

His twin-brother, who died when he was a day old, his mother had called Grundy—just because, as she said, "Solomon an' Grundy b'longs together in de books."

When the wee black boy began to talk, he knew himself equally as Solomon or Crow, and so, when asked his name, he would answer: "Sol'mon Crow," and Solomon Crow he thenceforth became.

Crow was ten years old now, and he was so very black and polished and thin, and had so peaked and bright a face, that no one who had any sense of humor could hear him called Crow without smiling.

Crow's mother, Tempest, had been a worker in her better days, but she had grown fatter and fatter until now she was so lazy and broad that her chief pleasure seemed to be sitting in her front door and gossiping with her neighbors over the fence, or in abusing or praising little Solomon, according to her mood.

Tempest had never been very honest. When, in the old days, she had hired out as cook and carried "her dinner" home at night, the basket on her arm had usually held enough for herself and Crow and a pig and the chickens—with some to give away. She had not meant Crow to understand, but the little fellow was wide awake, and his mother was his pattern.

But this is the boy's story. It seemed best to tell a little about his mother, so that, if he should some time do wrong things, we might all, writer and readers, be patient with him. He had been poorly taught. If we could not trace our honesty back to our mothers, how many of us would love the truth?

Crow's mother loved him very much—she thought. She would knock down any one who even blamed him for anything. Indeed, when things went well, she would sometimes go sound asleep in the door with her fat arm around him—very much as the mother-cat beside her lay half dozing while she licked her baby kitten.

But if Crow was awkward or forgot anything—or didn't bring home money enough—her abuse was worse than any mother-cat's claws.

One of her worst taunts on such occasions was about like this: "Well, you is a low-down nigger, I must say. Nobody, to look at you, would b'lieve you was twin to a angel!"

Or, "How you reckon yo' angel-twin feels ef he's a-lookin' at you now?"

Crow had great reverence for his little lost mate. Indeed, he feared the displeasure of this other self, who, he believed, watched him from the skies, quite as much as the anger of God. Sad to say, the good Lord, whom most children love as a kind, heavenly Father, was to poor little Solomon Crow only a terrible, terrible punisher of wrong, and the little boy trembled at His very name. He seemed to hear God's anger in the thunder or the wind; but in the blue sky, the faithful stars, the opening flowers and singing birds—in all loving-kindness and friendship—he never saw a heavenly Father's love.

He knew that some things were right and others wrong. He knew that it was right to go out and earn dimes to buy the things needed in the cabin, but he equally knew it was wrong to get this money dishonestly. Crow was a very shrewd little boy, and he made money honestly in a number of ways that only a wide-awake boy would think about.

When fig season came, in hot summer-time, he happened to notice that beautiful ripe figs were drying up on the tip-tops of some great trees in a neighboring yard, where a stout old gentleman and his old wife lived alone, and he began to reflect.

"If I could des git a-holt o' some o' dem fine sugar figs dat's a-swivelin' up every day on top o' dem trees, I'd meck a heap o' money peddlin' 'em on de street." And even while he thought this thought he licked his lips. There were, no doubt, other attractions about the figs for a very small boy with a very sweet tooth.

On the next morning after this, Crow rang the front gate-bell of the yard where the figs were growing.

"Want a boy to pick figs on sheers?" That was all he said to the fat old gentleman who had stepped around the house in answer to his ring.

Crow's offer was timely.

Old Mr. Cary was red in the face and panting even yet from reaching up into the mouldy, damp lower limbs of his fig-trees, trying to gather a dishful for breakfast.

"Come in," he said, mopping his forehead as he spoke.

"Pick on shares, will you?"

"Yassir."

"Even?"

"Yassir."

"Promise never to pick any but the very ripe figs?"

"Yassir."

"Honest boy?"

"Yassir."

"Turn in, then; but wait a minute."

He stepped aside into the house, returning presently with two baskets.

"Here," he said, presenting them both. "These are pretty nearly of a size. Go ahead, now, and let's see what you can do."

Needless to say, Crow proved a great success as fig-picker. The very sugary figs that old Mr. Cary had panted for and reached for in vain lay bursting with sweetness on top of both baskets.

The old gentleman and his wife were delighted, and the boy was quickly engaged to come every morning.

And this was how Crow went into the fig business.

Crow was a likable boy—"so bright and handy and nimble"—and the old people soon became fond of him.

They noticed that he always handed in the larger of the two baskets, keeping the smaller for himself. This seemed not only honest, but generous.

And generosity is a winning virtue in the very needy—as winning as it is common. The very poor are often great of heart.

But this is not a safe fact upon which to found axioms.

All God's poor are not educated up to the point of even small, fine honesties, and the so-called "generous" are not always "just" or honest.

And—

Poor little Solomon Crow! It is a pity to have to write it, but his weak point was exactly that he was not quite honest. He wanted to be, just because his angel-twin might be watching him, and he was afraid of thunder. But Crow was so anxious to be "smart" that he had long ago begun doing "tricky" things. Even the men working the roads had discovered this. In eating Crow's "fresh-boiled crawfish" or "shrimps," they would often come across one of the left-overs of yesterday's supply, mixed in with the others; and a yesterday's shrimp is full of stomach-ache and indigestion. So that business suffered.

In the fig business the ripe ones sold well; but when one of Crow's customers offered to buy all he would bring of green ones for preserving, Crow began filling his basket with them and distributing a top layer of ripe ones carefully over them. His lawful share of the very ripe he also carried away—in his little bread-basket.

This was all very dishonest, and Crow knew it. Still he did it many times.

And then—and this shows how one sin leads to another—and then, one day—oh, Solomon Crow, I'm ashamed to tell it on you!—one day he noticed that there were fresh eggs in the hen-house nests, quite near the fig-trees. Now, if there was anything Crow liked, it was a fried egg—two fried eggs. He always said he wanted two on his plate at once, looking at him like a pair of round eyes, "an' when dey reco'nizes me," he would say, "den I eats 'em up."

Why not slip a few of these tempting eggs into the bottom of the basket and cover them up with ripe figs?

And so—,

One day, he did it.

He had stopped at the dining-room door that day and was handing in the larger basket, as usual, when old Mr. Cary, who stood there, said, smiling:

"No, give us the smaller basket to-day, my boy. It's our turn to be generous."

He extended his hand as he spoke.

Crow tried to answer, but he could not. His mouth felt as dry and stiff and hard as a chip, and he suddenly began to open it wide and shut it slowly, like a chicken with the gapes.

Mr. Cary kept his hand out waiting, but still Crow stood as if paralyzed, gaping and swallowing.

Finally, he began to blink. And then he stammered:

"I ain't p-p-p-ertic'lar b-b-bout de big basket. D-d-d-de best figs is in y'all's pickin'—in dis, de big basket."

Crow's appearance was conviction itself. Without more ado, Mr. Cary grasped his arm firmly and fairly lifted him into the room.

"Now, set those baskets down." He spoke sharply.

The boy obeyed.

"Here! empty the larger one on this tray. That's it. All fine, ripe figs. You've picked well for us. Now turn the other one out."

At this poor Crow had a sudden relapse of the dry gapes. His arm fell limp and he looked as if he might tumble over.

"Turn 'em out!" The old gentleman shrieked in so thunderous a tone that Crow jumped off his feet, and, seizing the other basket with his little shaking paws, he emptied it upon the heap of figs.

Old Mrs. Cary had come in just in time to see the eggs roll out of the basket, and for a moment she and her husband looked at each other. And then they turned to the boy.

When she spoke her voice was so gentle that Crow, not understanding, looked quickly into her face:

"Let me take him into the library, William. Come, my boy."

Her tone was so soft, so sorrowful and sympathetic, that Crow felt as he followed her as if, in the hour of his deepest disgrace, he had found a friend; and when presently he stood in a great square room before a high arm-chair, in which a white-haired old lady sat looking at him over her gold-rimmed spectacles and talking to him as he had never been spoken to in all his life before, he felt as if he were in a great court before a judge who didn't understand half how very bad little boys were.

She asked him a good many questions—some very searching ones, too—all of which Crow answered as best he could, with his very short breath.

His first feeling had been of pure fright. But when he found he was not to be abused, not beaten or sent to jail, he began to wonder.

Little Solomon Crow, ten years old, in a Christian land, was hearing for the first time in his life that God loved him—loved him even now in his sin and disgrace, and wanted him to be good.

He listened with wandering eyes at first, half expecting the old gentleman, Mr. Cary, to appear suddenly at the door with a whip or a policeman with a club. But after a while he kept his eyes steadily upon the lady's face.

"Has no one ever told you, Solomon"—she had always called him Solomon, declaring that Crow was not a fit name for a boy who looked as he did—it was altogether "too personal"—"has no one ever told you, Solomon," she said, "that God loves all His little children, and that you are one of these children?"

"No, ma'am," he answered, with difficulty. And then, as if catching at something that might give him a little standing, he added, quickly—so quickly that he stammered again:

"B-b-b-but I knowed I was twin to a angel. I know dat. An' I knows ef my angel twin seen me steal dem aigs he'll be mightly ap' to tell Gord to strike me down daid."

Of course he had to explain then about the "angel twin," and the old lady talked to him for a long time. And then together they knelt down. When at last they came out of the library she held the boy's hand and led him to her husband.

"Are you willing to try him again, William?" she asked. "He has promised to do better."

Old Mr. Cary cleared his throat and laid down his paper.

"Don't deserve it," he began; "dirty little thief." And then he turned to the boy: "What have you got on, sir?"

His voice was really quite terrible.

"N-n-n-nothin'; only but des my b-b-b-briches an' jacket, an'—an'—an' skin," Crow replied, between gasps.

"How many pockets?"

"Two," said Crow.

"Turn 'em out!"

Crow drew out his little rust-stained pockets, dropping a few old nails and bits of twine upon the floor as he did so.

"Um—h'm! Well, now, I'll tell you. *You're a dirty little thief,* as I said before. And I'm going to treat you as one. If you wear those pockets hanging out, or rip 'em out, and come in here before you leave every day dressed just as you are—pants and jacket and skin—and empty out your basket for us before you go, until I'm satisfied you'll do better, you can come."

The old lady looked at her husband as if she thought him pretty hard on a very small boy. But she said nothing.

Crow glanced appealingly at her before answering. And then he said, seizing his pocket:

"Is you got air pair o' scissors, lady?"

Mrs. Cary wished her husband would relent even while she brought the scissors, but he only cried:

"Out with 'em!"

"Suppose you cut them out yourself, Solomon," she interposed, kindly, handing him the scissors. "You'll have all this work to do yourself. We can't make you good."

When, after several awkward efforts, Crow finally put the coarse little pockets in her hands, there were tears in her eyes, and she tried to hide them as she leaned over and gathered up his treasures—three nails, a string, a broken top, and a half-eaten chunk of cold corn-bread. As she handed them to him she said: "And I'll lay the pockets away for you, Solomon, and when we see that you are an honest boy I'll sew them back for you myself."

As she spoke she rose, divided the figs evenly between the two baskets, and handed one to Crow.

If there ever was a serious little black boy on God's beautiful earth it was little Solomon Crow as he balanced his basket of figs on his head that day and went slowly down the garden walk and out the great front gate.

The next few weeks were not without trial to the boy. Old Mr. Cary continued very stern, even following him daily to the *banquette*, as if he dare not trust him to go out alone. And when he closed the iron gate after him he would say in a tone that was awfully solemn:

"Good-mornin', sir!"

That was all.

Little Crow dreaded that walk to the gate more than all the rest of the ordeal. And yet, in a way, it gave him courage. He was at least worth while, and with time and patience he would win back the lost faith of the friends who were kind to him even while they could not trust him. They were, indeed, kind and generous in many ways, both to him and his unworthy mother.

Fig-time was soon nearly over, and, of course, Crow expected a dismissal; but it was Mr. Cary himself who set these fears at rest by proposing to him to come daily to blacken his boots and to keep the garden-walk in order for regular wages.

"But," he warned him, in closing, "don't you show your face here with a pocket on you. If your heavy pants have any in 'em, rip 'em out." And then he added, severely: "You've been a very bad boy."

"Yassir," answered Crow, "I know I is. I been a heap wusser boy'n you knowed I was, too."

"What's that you say, sir?"

Crow repeated it. And then he added, for full confession:

"I picked green figs heap o' days, and kivered 'em up wid ripe ones, an' sol' 'em to a white 'oman fur perserves." There was something desperate in the way he blurted it all out.

"The dickens you did! And what are you telling me for?"

He eyed the boy keenly as he put the question.

At this Crow fairly wailed aloud: "'Caze I ain't gwine do it no mo'." And throwing his arms against the door-frame he buried his face in them, and he sobbed as if his little heart would break.

For a moment old Mr. Cary seemed to have lost his voice, and then he said, in a voice quite new to Crow:

"I don't believe you will, sir—I don't believe you will." And in a minute he said, still speaking gently: "Come here, boy."

Still weeping aloud, Crow obeyed.

"Tut, tut! No crying!" he began. "Be a man—be a man. And if you stick to it, before Christmas comes, we'll see about those pockets, and you can walk into the new year with your head up. But look sharp! Good-bye, now!"

For the first time since the boy's fall Mr. Cary did not follow him to the gate. Maybe this was the beginning of trust. Slight a thing as it was, the boy took comfort in it.

At last it was Christmas eve. Crow was on the back "gallery" putting a final polish on a pair of boots. He was nearly done, and his heart was beginning to sink, when the old lady came and stood near him. There was a very hopeful twinkle in her eye as she said, presently: "I wonder what our little shoeblack, who has been trying so hard to be good, would like to have for his Christmas gift?"

But Crow only blinked while he polished the faster.

"Tell me, Solomon," she insisted. "If you had one wish to-day, what would it be?"

The boy wriggled nervously. And then he said:

"You knows, lady. Needle—an' thrade—an'—an'—you knows, lady. Pockets."

"Well, pockets it shall be. Come into my room when you get through."

Old Mrs. Cary sat beside the fire reading as he went in. Seeing him, she nodded, smiling, towards the bed, upon which Crow saw a brand-new suit of clothes—coat, vest, and breeches—all spread out in a row.

"There, my boy," she said; "there are your pockets."

Crow had never in all his life owned a full new suit of clothes. All his "new" things had been second-hand, and for a moment he could not quite believe his eyes; but he went quickly to the bed and began passing his hands over the clothes. Then he ventured to take up the vest—and to turn it over. And now he began to find pockets.

"Three pockets in de ves'—two in de pants—an'—an' fo', no five, no six—six pockets in de coat!"

He giggled nervously as he thrust his little black fingers into one and then another. And then, suddenly overcome with a sense of the situation, he turned to Mrs. Cary, and, in a voice that trembled a little, said:

"Is you sho' you ain't 'feerd to trus' me wid all deze pockets, lady?"

It doesn't take a small boy long to slip into a new suit of clothes. And when a ragged urchin disappeared behind the head of the great old "four-poster" to-day, it seemed scarcely a minute before a trig, "tailor-made boy" strutted out from the opposite side, hands deep in pockets—breathing hard.

As Solomon Crow strode up and down the room, radiant with joy, he seemed for the moment quite unconscious of any one's presence. But presently he stopped, looked involuntarily upward a minute, as if he felt himself observed from above. Then, turning to the old people, who stood together before the mantel, delightedly watching him, he said:

"Bet you my angel twin ain't ashamed, ef he's a-lookin' down on me to-day."

THE TWO TIMS

THE TWO TIMS

As the moon sent a white beam through the little square window of old Uncle Tim's cabin, it formed a long panel of light upon its smoke-stained wall, bringing into clear view an old banjo hanging upon a rusty nail. Nothing else in the small room was clearly visible. Although it was Christmas eve, there was no fire upon the broad hearth, and from the open door came the odor of honeysuckles and of violets. Winter is often in Louisiana only a name given by courtesy to the months coming between autumn and spring, out of respect to the calendar; and so it was this year.

Sitting in the open doorway, his outline lost in the deep shadows of the vine, was old Uncle Tim, while, upon the floor at his side lay little Tim, his grandson. The boy lay so still that in the dim half-light he seemed a part of the floor furnishings, which were, in fact, an old cot, two crippled stools, a saddle, and odds and ends of broken harness, and bits of rope.

Neither the old man nor the boy had spoken for a long time, and while they gazed intently at the old banjo hanging in the panel of light, the thoughts of both were tinged with sadness. The grandfather was nearly seventy years old, and little Tim was but ten; but they were great chums. The little boy's father had died while he was too young to remember, leaving little Tim to a step-mother, who brought him to his grandfather's home, where he had been ever since, and the attachment quickly formed between the two had grown and strengthened with the years.

Old Uncle Tim was very poor, and his little cabin was small and shabby; and yet neither hunger nor cold had ever come in an unfriendly way to visit it. The tall plantation smoke-house threw a friendly shadow over the tiny hut every evening just before the sun went down—a shadow that seemed a promise at close of each day that the poor home should not be forgotten. Nor was it. Some days the old man was able to limp into the field and cut a load of cabbages for the hands, or to prepare seed potatoes for planting, so that, as he expressed it, "each piece 'll have one eye ter grow wid an' another ter look on an' see dat everything goes right."

And then Uncle Tim was brimful of a good many valuable things with which he was very generous—*advice*, for instance.

He could advise with wisdom upon any number of subjects, such as just at what time of the moon to make soap so that it would "set" well, how to find a missing shoat, or the right spot to dig for water.

These were all valuable services; yet cabbages were not always ready to be cut, potato-planting was not always in season. Often for weeks not a hog would stray off. Only once in a decade a new well was wanted; and as to soap-making, it could occur only once during each moon at most.

It is true that between times Uncle Tim gave copious warnings *not* to make soap, which was quite a saving of effort and good material.

But whether he was cutting seed potatoes, or advising, or only playing on his banjo, as he did incessantly between times, his rations came to the little cabin with clock-like regularity. They came just as regularly as old Tim *had worked* when he was young, as regularly as little Tim *would* when he should grow up, as it is a pity daily rations cannot always come to such feeble ones as, whether in their first or second childhood, are able to render only the service of willingness.

And so we see that the two Tims, as they were often called, had no great anxieties as to their living, although they were very poor.

The only thing in the world that the old man held as a personal possession was his old banjo. It was the one thing the little boy counted on as a precious future property. Often, at all hours of the day or evening, old Tim could be seen sitting before the cabin, his arms around the boy, who stood between his knees, while, with eyes closed, he ran his withered fingers over the strings, picking out the tunes that best recalled the stories of olden days that he loved to tell into the little fellow's ear. And sometimes, holding the banjo steady, he would invite little Tim to try his tiny hands at picking the strings.

"Look out how you snap 'er too sudden!" he would exclaim if the little fingers moved too freely. "Look out, I say! Dis ain't none o' yo' pick-me-up-hit-an'-miss banjos, she ain't! An' you mus' learn ter treat 'er wid rispec', caze, when yo' ole gran'dad dies, she gwine be yo' banjo, an' stan' in his place ter yer!"

And then little Tim, confronted with the awful prospect of death and inheritance, would take a long breath, and, blinking his eyes, drop his hands at his side, saying, "You play 'er gran'dad."

But having once started to speak, the old man was seldom brief, and so he would continue: "It's true dis ole banjo she's livin' in a po' nigger cabin wid a ole black marster an' a new one comin' on blacker yit. (You taken dat arter yo' gran'mammy, honey. She warn't dis heah muddy-brown color like I is. She was a heap purtier and clairer black.) Well, I say, if dis ole banjo *is* livin' wid po' ignunt black folks, I wants you ter know she was *born white*.

"Don't look at me so cuyus, honey. I know what I say. I say she was *born white*. Dat is, she *de*scended ter me *f'om* white folks. My marster bought 'er ter learn on when we was boys together. An' he took *book lessons* on 'er too, an' dat's how come I say she ain't none o' yo' common pick-up-my-strings-any-which-er-way banjos. She's been played by note music in her day, she is, an' she can answer a book note des as true as any *pi*anner a pusson ever listened at—ef anybody know how ter tackle 'er. Of co'se, ef you des tackle 'er p'omiskyus she ain't gwine bother 'erse'f ter play 'cordin' ter rule; but—

"Why, boy, dis heah banjo she's done serenaded all de a'stocercy on dis river 'twix' here an' de English Turn in her day. Yas, she is. An' all dat expeunce is in 'er breast now; she 'ain't forgot it, an' ef air pusson dat know all dem ole book chunes was ter take 'er up an' call fur 'em, she'd give 'em eve'y one des as true as ever yit.

"An' yer know, baby, I'm a-tellin' you all dis," he would say, in closing—"I'm a-tellin' you all dis caze arter while, when I die, she gwine be *yo'* banjo, 'n' I wants you ter know all 'er ins an' outs."

And as he stopped, the little boy would ask, timidly, "Please, sir, gran'dad, lemme tote 'er an' hang 'er up. I'll step keerful." And taking each step with the utmost precision, and holding the long banjo aloft in his arms as if it were made of egg-shells, little Tim would climb the stool and hang the precious thing in its place against the cabin wall.

Such a conversation had occurred to-day, and as the lad had taken the banjo from him the old man had added:

"I wouldn't be s'prised, baby, ef 'fo' another year passes dat'll be *yo' banjo*, caze I feels mighty weak an' painful some days."

This was in the early evening, several hours before the scene with which this little story opens. As night came on and the old man sat in the doorway, he did not notice that little Tim, in stretching himself upon the floor, as was his habit, came nearer than usual—so near, indeed, that, extending his little foot, he rested it against his grandfather's body, too lightly to be felt, and yet sensibly enough to satisfy his own affectionate impulse. And so he was lying when the moon rose and covered the old banjo with its light. He felt very serious as he gazed upon it, standing out so distinctly in the dark room. Some day it would be his; but the dear old grandfather would not be there, his chair would be always empty. There would be nobody in the little cabin but just little Tim and the banjo. He was too young to think of other changes. The ownership of the coveted treasure promised only death and utter loneliness. But presently the light passed off the wall on to the floor. It was creeping over to where little Tim lay, but he did not know it, and after blinking awhile at long intervals, and moving his foot occasionally to reassure himself of his grandfather's presence, he fell suddenly sound asleep.

While these painful thoughts were filling little Tim's mind the old man had studied the bright panel on the wall with equal interest—and pain. By the very nature of things he could not leave the banjo to the boy and witness his pleasure in the possession.

"She's de onlies' thing I got ter leave 'im, but I does wush't I could see him git 'er an' be at his little elbow ter show 'im all 'er ways," he said, half audibly. "Dis heah way o' leavin' things ter folks when you die, it sounds awful high an' mighty, but look ter me like hit's po' satisfaction some ways. Po' little Tim! Now what he gwine do anyhow when I draps off?—nothin' but step-folks ter take keer of 'im—step-mammy an' step-daddy an' 'bout a dozen step brothers an' sisters, an' not even me heah ter show 'im how ter conduc' 'is banjo. De ve'y time he need me de mos' ter show 'im her ins an' outs I won't be nowhars about, an' yit—"

As the old man's thoughts reached this point a sudden flare of light across the campus showed that the first bonfire was lighted.

There was to be a big dance to-night in the open space in front of the sugar-house, and the lighting of the bonfires surrounding the spot was the announcement that it was time for everybody to come. It was Uncle Tim's signal to take down the banjo and tune up, for there was no more important instrument in the plantation string-band than this same old banjo.

As he turned backward to wake little Tim he hesitated a moment, looking lovingly upon the little sleeping figure, which the moon now covered with a white rectangle of light. As his eyes rested upon the boy's face something, a confused memory of his last waking anxiety perhaps, brought a slight quiver to his lips, as if he might cry in his sleep, while he muttered the word "gran'dad."

Old Uncle Tim had been trying to get himself to the point of doing something which it was somehow hard to do, but this tremulous lisping of his own name settled the question.

Hobbling to his feet, he wended his way as noiselessly as possible to where the banjo hung, and, carrying it to the sleeping boy, laid it gently, with trembling fingers, upon his arm.

Then, first silently regarding him a moment, he called out, "Weck up, Tim, my man! Weck up!"

As he spoke, a loud and continuous explosion of fire-crackers—the opening of active festivities in the campus—startled the boy quite out of his nap.

He was frightened and dazed for a minute, and then, seeing the banjo beside him and his grandfather's face so near, he exclaimed: "What's all dis, gran'dad? Whar me?"

The old man's voice was pretty husky as he answered: "You right heah wid me, boy, an' dat banjo, hit's yo' Christmas gif', honey."

Little Tim cast an agonized look upon the old man's face, and threw himself into his arms. "Is you gwine die now, gran'dad?" he sobbed, burying his face upon his bosom.

Old Tim could not find voice at once, but presently he chuckled, nervously: "Humh! humh! No, boy, I ain't gwine die yit—not till my time comes, please Gord. But dis heah's Christmas, honey, an' I thought I'd gi'e you de ole banjo whiles I was living so's I could—so's you could—so's we could have pleasure out'n 'er bofe together, yer know, honey. Dat is, f'om dis time on she's *yo' banjo*, an' when I wants ter play on 'er, you *can loan 'er ter me*."

"An'—an' you—you *sho'* you ain't gwine die, gran'dad?"

"I ain't sho' o' nothin', honey, but I 'ain't got no *notion* o' dyin'—not to-night. We gwine ter de dance now, you an' me, an' I gwine play de banjo—*dat is ef you'll loan 'er ter me, baby*."

Tim wanted to laugh, and it seemed sheer contrariness for him to cry, but somehow the tears would come, and the lump in his throat, and try hard as he might, he couldn't get his head higher than his grandfather's coat-sleeve or his arms from around his waist. He hardly knew why he still wept, and yet when presently he sobbed, "But, gran'dad, I'm 'feered you *mought* die," the old man understood.

Certainly, even if he were not going to die now, giving away the old banjo seemed like a preparation for death. Was it not, in fact, a formal confession that he was nearing the end of his days? Had not this very feeling made it hard for him to part with it? The boy's grief at the thought touched him deeply, and lifting the little fellow upon his knee, he said, fondly:

"*Don't* fret, honey. *Don't* let Christmas find yon cryin'. I tell you what I say let's do. I ain't gwine gi'e you de banjo, not yit, caze, des as you say, I *mought* die; but I tell you what I gwine do. I gwine take you in pardners in it wid me. She ain't *mine* an' she ain't *yoze*, and yit she's *bofe of us's*. You see, boy? *She's ourn!* An' when I wants ter play on 'er *I'll play*, an' when you wants 'er, why, you teck 'er—on'y be a *leetle* bit keerful at fust, honey."

"An' kin I ca'y 'er behine de cabin, whar you can't see how I'm a-holdin' 'er, an' play anyway I choose?"

Old Tim winced a little at this, but he had not given grudgingly.

"Cert'n'y," he answered. "Why not? Git up an' play 'er in de middle o' de night ef you want ter, on'y, of co'se, be keerful how you reach 'er down, so's you won't jolt 'er too sudden. An' now, boy, hand 'er heah an' lemme talk to yer a little bit."

When little Tim lifted the banjo from the floor his face fairly beamed with joy, although in the darkness no one saw it, for the shaft of light had passed beyond him now. Handing the banjo to his grandfather, he slipped naturally back of it into his accustomed place in his arms.

"Dis heah's a fus'-class thing ter work off bad tempers wid," the old man began, tightening the strings as he spoke. "Now ef one o' deze mule tempers ever take a-holt of yer in de foot, dat foot 'll be mighty ap' ter do some kickin'; an' ef it seizes a-holt o' yo' han', dat little fis' 'll be purty sho ter strike out an' do some damage; an' ef it jump onter yo' tongue, hit 'll mighty soon twis' it into sayin' bad language. But ef you'll teck hol' o' dis ole banjo des as quick as you feel de badness rise up in you, *an' play*, you'll scare de evil temper away so bad it *daresn't come back*. Ef it done settled *too strong* in yo' tongue, run it off wid a song; an' ef yo' feet's git a kickin' spell on 'em, *dance it off*; an' ef you feel it in yo' han', des run fur de banjo an' play de sweetes' chune you know, an' fus' thing you know all yo' madness 'll be gone.

"She 'ain't got no mouf, but she can talk ter you, all de same; an' she 'ain't got no head, but she can reason wid you. An' while ter look at 'er she's purty nigh all belly, she don't eat a crumb. Dey ain't a greedy bone in 'er.

"An' I wants you ter ricollec' dat I done guv 'er to you—dat is, *yo' sheer in 'er*, caze she's *mine* too, you know. I done guv you a even sheer in 'er, des *caze you an' me is gran'daddy an' gran'son*.

"Dis heah way o' dyin' an' *leavin'* prop'ty, hit mought suit white folks, but it don't become our complexioms, some way; an' de mo' I thought about havin' to die ter give de onlies' gran'son I got de onlies' *prop'ty* I got, de *miser'bler I got*, tell I couldn't stan' it no mo'."

Little Tim's throat choked up again, and he rolled his eyes around and swallowed twice before he answered: "An' I—I was miser'ble too, gran'dad. I used ter des look at 'er hangin' 'g'inst de wall, an' think about me maybe playin' 'er, an' you—you not—not nowhar in sight—an'—an' some days seem like *I—I des hated 'er*."

"Yas, baby, I know. But now you won't hate 'er no mo', boy; an' ef you die fus'—some time, you know, baby, little boys *does die*—an' ef you go fus', I'll teck good keer o' yo' sheer in 'er; an' ef I go, you mus' look out fur my sheer. An' long as we bofe live—well, I'll look out fur 'er voice—keep 'er th'oat strings in order; an' you see dat she don't git ketched out in bad comp'ny, or in de rain, an' take cold.

"Come on now. Wash yo' little face, and let's go ter de dance. Gee-man! Lis'n at de fire-crackers callin' us. Come on. Dat's right. Pack 'er on yo' shoulder like a man."

And so the two Tims start off to the Christmas festival, young Tim bearing his precious burden proudly ahead, while the old man follows slowly behind, chuckling softly.

"Des think how much time I done los', not takin' 'im in pardners befo', an' he de onlies' gran'son I got!"

While little Tim, walking cautiously so as not to trip in the uneven path, turns presently and calls back:

"Gran'dad, I reckon we done walked half de way, now. I done toted 'er *my* sheer. Don't you want me ter tote 'er *yo' sheer*?"

And the old man answers, with another chuckle, "Go on, honey."

THE FREYS' CHRISTMAS PARTY

THE FREYS' CHRISTMAS PARTY

There was a great sensation in the old Coppenole house three days before Christmas. The Freys, who lived on the third floor, were going to give a Christmas dinner party, and all the other tenants were invited.

Such a thing had never happened before, and, as Miss Penny told her canary-birds while she filled their seed-cups, it was "like a clap of thunder out of a clear sky."

The Frey family, consisting of a widow and her brood of half a dozen children, were as poor as any of the tenants in the old building, for wasn't the mother earning a scant living as a beginner in newspaper work? Didn't the Frey children do every bit of the house-work, not to mention little outside industries by which the older ones earned small incomes? Didn't Meg send soft gingerbread to the Christian Woman's Exchange for sale twice a week, and Ethel find time, with all her studies, to paint butterflies on Swiss aprons for fairs or fêtes?

Didn't everybody know that Conrad, now but thirteen, was a regular solicitor for orders for Christmas-trees, palmetto palms, and gray moss from the woods for decorative uses on holiday occasions?

The idea of people in such circumstances as these giving dinner parties! It was almost incredible; but it was true, for tiny notes of invitation tied with rose-colored ribbons had been flying over the building all the afternoon. The Frey twins, Felix and Félicie, both barefoot, had carried one to each door.

They were written with gold ink on pink paper. A water-colored butterfly was poised in midair somewhere on each one, and at the left lower end were the mysterious letters "R.S.V.P."

The old Professor who lived in the room next the Frey kitchen got one, and Miss Penny, who occupied the room beyond. So did Mademoiselle Guyosa, who made paper flowers, and the mysterious little woman of the last, worst room in the house—a tiny figure whose face none of her neighbors had ever seen, but who had given her name to the baker and milkman as "Mamzelle St. John."

And there were others. Madame Coraline, the fortune-teller, who rented the hall room on the second floor, was perhaps more surprised at her invitation than any of the rest. No one ever asked her anywhere. Even the veiled ladies who sometimes visited her darkened chamber always tiptoed up the steps as if they were half ashamed of going there.

The twins had a time getting her to come to the door to receive the invitation, and after vainly rapping several times, they had finally brought a parasol and hammered upon the horseshoe tacked upon the door, until at last it opened just about an inch. And then she was invited.

But, indeed, it is time to be telling how the party originated.

It had been the habit of the Frey children, since they could remember, to save up spare coins all the year for a special fund which they called "Christmas money."

The old fashion of spending these small amounts in presents for one another had long ago given place to the better one—more in the Christmas spirit—of using it to brighten the day for some one less blessed than themselves.

It is true that on the Christmas before the one of this story they had broken the rule, or only strained it, perhaps, to buy a little stove for their mother's room.

But a rule that would not stretch enough to take in such a home need would be a poor one indeed.

This year they had had numerous schemes, but somehow none had seemed to appeal to the stockholders in the Christmas firm, and so they had finally called a meeting on the subject.

It was at this meeting that Meg, fourteen years old, having taken the floor, said: "Well, it seems to *me* that the *worst* kind of a Christmas must be a lonely one. Just think how nearly all the roomers in this house spent last Christmas—most of 'em sittin' by their lone selves in their rooms, and some of 'em just eatin' every-day things! The Professor hadn't a thing but Bologna-sausage and crackers. *I know—'cause I peeped.* An' now, whatever you all are goin' to do with *your* money, *mine's* goin' right into this house, to the roomers—*some way.*"

"If we knew what we could do, Meg?" said Ethel.

"If we knew what we could do or *how we could do it*," interrupted Conrad, "why, I'd give my eighty-five cents in a minute. I'd give it to the old Professor to have his curls cut."

Conrad was a true-hearted fellow, but he was full of mischief.

"Shame on you, Buddy!" said Meg, who was thoroughly serious. "Can't you be in earnest for just a minute?"

"I am in earnest, Meg. I think your scheme is bully—if it could be worked; but the Professor wouldn't take our money any more'n we'd take his."

"Neither would any of them." This was Ethel's first real objection.

"Who's goin' to offer 'em money?" rejoined Meg.

"I tell you what we *might* do, maybe," Conrad suggested, dubiously. "We *might* buy a lot of fine grub, an' send it in to 'em sort o' mysteriously. How'd that do?"

"'Twouldn't do at all," Meg replied. "The idea! Who'd enjoy the finest Christmas dinner in the world by his lone self, with nothin' but a lookin'-glass to look into and holler 'Merry Christmas' to?"

Conrad laughed. "Well, the Professor's little cracked glass wouldn't be much of a comfort to a hungry fellow. It gives you two mouths."

Conrad was nothing if not facetious.

"There you are again, Buddy! *Do* be serious for once." And then she added, desperately, "The thing *I* want to do is to *invite* 'em."

"Invite!"

"Who?"

"What?"

"When?"

"How?"

"Where?"

Such was the chorus that greeted Meg's astounding proposition.

"Why, I say," she explained, nothing daunted, "let's put all our Christmas money together and get the very best dinner we can, and invite all the roomers to come and eat it with us. *Now I've said it!* And I ain't foolin', either."

"And we haven't a whole table-cloth to our names, Meg Frey, and you know it!" It was Ethel who spoke again.

"And what's that got to do with it, Sisty? We ain't goin' to eat the cloth. Besides, can't we set the dish-mats over the holes? 'Twouldn't be the first time."

"But, Meg, dearie, you surely are not proposing to invite company to dine in the kitchen, are you? And who'd cook the dinner, not to mention buying it?"

"Well, now, listen, Sisty, dear. The dinner that's in my mind isn't a society-column dinner like those Momsy writes about, and those we are going to invite don't wear out much table-linen at home. And they cook their own dinners, too, most of 'em—exceptin' when they eat 'em in the French Market, with a Chinaman on one side of 'em and an Indian on the other.

"*I'm* goin' to cook *ours*, and as for eatin' in the kitchen, why, we don't need to. Just see how warm it is! The frost hasn't even nipped the banana leaves over there in the square. And Buddy can pull the table out on the big back gallery, an' we'll hang papa's old gray soldier blanket for a portière to keep the Quinettes from lookin' in; and, Sisty, you can write the invitations an' paint butterflies on 'em."

Ethel's eyes for the first time sparkled with interest, but she kept silent, and Meg continued:

"An' Buddy'll bring in a lot of gray moss and *latanier* to dec'rate with, an'—"

"An' us'll wait on the table!"

"Yes, us'll wait on the table!" cried the twins.

"But," added Felix in a moment, "you mus'n't invite Miss Penny, Meg, 'cause if you do F'lissy an' me'll be thest shore to disgrace the party a-laughin'. She looks thest ezzac'ly like a canary-bird, an' Buddy has tooken her off till we thest die a-laughin' every time we see her. I think she's raised canaries till she's a sort o' half-canary herself. Don't let's invite her, Sisty."

"And don't you think Miss Penny would enjoy a slice of Christmas turkey as well as the rest of us, Felix?"

"No; I fink she ought to eat canary-seed and fish-bone," chirped in Dorothea.

Dorothea was only five, and this from her was so funny that even Meg laughed.

"An' Buddy says he knows she sleeps perched on the towel-rack, 'cause they ain't a sign of a bed in her room."

The three youngest were fairly choking with laughter now. But the older ones had soon grown quite serious in consulting about all the details of the matter, and even making out a conditional list of guests.

When they came to the fortune-teller, both Ethel and Conrad hesitated, but Meg, true to her first impulse, had soon put down opposition by a single argument.

"It seems to me she's the special one *to* invite to a Christmas party like ours," she pleaded. "The lonesomer an' horrider they are, the more they belong, an' the more they'll enjoy it, too."

"Accordin' to that," said Conrad, "the whole crowd ought to have a dizzy good time, for they're about as fine a job lot of lonesomes as I ever struck. And as for beauty! 'Vell, my y'ung vriends, how you was to-morrow?'" he continued, thrusting his thumbs into his armholes and strutting in imitation of the old Professor.

"'SHE OUGHT TO EAT CANARY-SEED AND FISH-BONE'"

Meg was almost out of patience. "Do hush, Buddy, an' let's talk business. First of all, we have to put it to vote to see whether we *want* to have the party or not."

"I ain't a-goin' to give my money to no such a ugly ol' party," cried Felix. "I want pretty little girls with curls an' wreafs on to my party."

"An' me, too. I want a heap o' pretty little girls with curls an' wreafs on—*to my party*," echoed Félicie.

"An' I want a organ-grinder to the party that gets my half o' our picayunes," insisted Felix.

"Yas, us wants a organ-grinder—an' a monkey, too—hey, F'lix?"

"Yes, an' a monkey, too. Heap o' monkeys!"

Meg was indeed having a hard time of it.

"You see, Conrad"—the use of that name meant reproof from Meg—"you see, Conrad, this all comes from your makin' fun of everybody. But of course we can get an organ-grinder if the little ones want him."

Ethel still seemed somewhat doubtful about the whole affair. Ethel was in the high-school. She had a lofty bridge to her nose. She was fifteen, and she never left off her final g's as the others did. These are, no doubt, some of the reasons why she was regarded as a sort of superior person in the family. If it had not been for the prospect of painting the cards, and a certain feeling of benevolence in the matter, it would have been hard for her to agree to the party at all. As it was, her voice had a note of mild protest as she said:

"It's going to cost a good deal, Meg. How much money have we? Let's count up. I have a dollar and eighty-five cents."

"And I've got two dollars," said Meg.

"How is it you always save the most? I haven't saved but ninety cents." Conrad spoke with a little real embarrassment as he laid his little pile of coins upon the table.

"I reckon it's 'cause I've got a regular plan, Buddy. I save a dime out of every dollar I get all through the year. It's the best way. And how much have you ponies got?"

"We've got seventy cents together, an' we've been a-whiskerin' in our ears about it, too. We don't want our money put-ed in the dinner with the rest. We want to see what we are givin'."

"Well, suppose you buy the fruit. Seventy cents 'll get bananas and oranges enough for the whole party."

"An' us wants to buy 'em ourselfs, too—hey, F'lix?"

"Yes, us wants to buy 'm ourselfs, too."

"And so you shall. And now all in favor of the party hold up their right hands."

All hands went up.

"Contr'ry, no!" Meg continued.

"Contr'ry, no!" echoed the twins.

"Hush! You mus'n't say that. That's just what they say at votin's."

"Gee-man-tally! But you girls 're awfully mixed," Conrad howled, with laughter. "They don't have any 'contr'ry no's' when they vote by holdin' up right hands. Besides, Dorothea held up her left hand, for I saw her."

"Which is quite correct, Mr. Smartie, since we all know that Dolly is left-handed. You meant to vote for the party, didn't you, dearie?" Meg added, turning to Dorothea.

For answer the little maid only bobbed her head, thrusting both hands behind her, as if afraid to trust them again.

"But I haven't got but thest a nickel," she ventured, presently. "F'lix says it'll buy salt."

"Salt!" said Conrad. "Well, I should smile! It would buy salt enough to pickle the whole party. Why, that little St. Johns woman goes out with a nickel an' lays in provisions. I've seen her do it."

"Shame on you, Buddy!"

"I'm not jokin', Meg. At least, I saw her buy a *quartie's* worth o' coffee and a *quartie's* worth o' sugar, an' then ask for *lagniappe* o' salt. Ain't that layin' in provisions? She uses a cigar-box for her pantry, too."

"Well," she protested, seriously, "what of it, Conrad? It doesn't take much for one very little person. Now, then, the party is voted for; but there's one more thing to be done before it can be really decided. We must ask Momsy's permission, of course. And that is goin' to be hard, because I don't want her to know about it. She has to be out reportin' festivals for the paper clear up to Christmas mornin', and if she knows about it, she'll worry over it. So I propose to ask her to let us give her a Christmas surprise, and not tell her what it is."

"And we know just what she'll say," Conrad interrupted; "she'll say, 'If you older children all agree upon anything, I'm sure it can't be very far wrong or foolish'—just as she did time we put up the stove in her room."

"Yes, I can hear her now," said Ethel. "But still we must *let* her say it before we do a single thing, because, you know, *she mightn't*. An' then where'd the party be?"

"It would be scattered around where it was last Christmas—where all the parties are that don't be," said Conrad. "They must be the ones we are always put down for, an' that's how we get left; eh, Sisty?"

"Never mind, Buddy; we won't get left, as you call it, this time, anyway—unless, of course, Momsy vetoes it."

"Vetoes what, children?"

They had been so noisy that they had not heard their mother's step on the creaking stairs.

Mrs. Frey carried her pencil and notes, and she looked tired, but she smiled indulgently as she repeated, "What am I to veto, dearies—or to approve?"

"It's a sequet! A Trismas sequet!"

"Yes, an' it's got owanges in it—"

"—An' bananas!"

"Hush, you ponies! And, Dolly, not another word!" Meg had resolutely taken the floor again.

"Momsy, we've been consulting about our Christmas money, and we've voted to ask you to let us do something with it, and not to tell you a thing about it, only "—and here she glanced for approval at Ethel and Conrad—"only we *ought* to tell you, Momsy, dear, that the surprise isn't for you this time."

And then Mrs. Frey, sweet mother that she was, made just the little speech they thought she would make, and when they had kissed her, and all, even to Ethel, who seemed now as enthusiastic as the others, caught hands and danced around the dinner table, she was glad she had consented.

It was such a delight to be able to supplement their scant Christmas prospects with an indulgence giving such pleasure.

"And I'm glad it isn't for me, children," she added, as soon as the hubbub gave her a hearing. "I'm very glad. You know you strained a point last year, and I'm sure you did right. My little stove has been a great comfort. But I am always certain of just as many home-made presents as I have children, and they are the ones I value. Dolly's lamp-lighters are not all used up yet, and if she *were* to give me another bundle this Christmas I shouldn't feel sorry. But our little Christmas *money* we want to send out on some loving mission. And, by-the-way, I have two dollars which may go with yours if you need it—if it will make some poor body's bed softer or his dinner better."

"Momsy's guessed!" Felix clapped his hands with delight.

"'Sh! Hush, Felix! Yes, Momsy, it'll do one of those things exactly," said Meg. "And now *I* say we'd better break up this meeting before the ponies tell the whole business."

"F'lix never telled a thing," chirped Félicie, always ready to defend her mate. "Did you, F'lixy? Momsy said 'dinner' herself."

"So I did, dear; but who is to get the dinner and why you are going to send it are things mother doesn't wish to know. And here are my two dollars. Now off to bed, the whole trundle-bed crowd, for I have a lot of copy to write to-night. Ethel may bring me a bite, and then sit beside me and write while I sip my tea and dictate and Meg puts the chickens to roost. And Conrad will keep quiet over his books. Just one kiss apiece and a hug for Dolly. Shoo now!"

So the party was decided.

The Frey home, although one of the poorest, was one of the happiest in New Orleans, for it was made up of cheery workers, even little Dorothea having her daily self-assumed tasks. Miss Dorothea, if you please, dusted the banisters round the porch every day, straightened the rows of shoes in mother's closet, folded the daily papers in the rack, and kept the one rug quite even with the front of the hearth. And this young lady had, furthermore, her regular income of five cents a week.

Of course her one nickel contributed to the party had been saved only a few hours, but Dorothea was only five, and the old yellow *praline* woman knew about her income, and came trudging all the way up the stairs each week on "pay-day."

Even after the invitations were sent it seemed to Dolly that the "party-day" would never come, for there were to be "three sleeps" before it should arrive.

It was Ethel's idea to send the cards early, so as to forestall any home preparation among the guests.

But all things come to him who waits—even Christmas. And so at last the great day arrived.

Nearly all the invited had accepted, and everything was very exciting; but the situation was not without its difficulties.

Even though she was out every day, it had been so hard to keep every tell-tale preparation out of Mrs. Frey's sight. But when she had found a pan of crullers on the top pantry shelf, or heard the muffled "gobble-gobble" of the turkey shut up in the old flour-barrel, or smelt invisible bananas and apples, she had been truly none the wiser, but had only said, "Bless their generous hearts! They are getting up a fine dinner to send to somebody."

Indeed, Mrs. Frey never got an inkling of the whole truth until she tripped up the stairs a half-hour before dinner on Christmas day to find the feast all spread.

The old mahogany table, extended to its full length, stood gorgeous in decorations of palmetto, moss, and flowers out upon the deep back porch, which was converted into a very pretty chamber by the hanging curtain of gray.

If she had any misgivings about it, she betrayed them by no single word or look, but there were bright red spots upon her usually pale cheeks as she passed, smiling, into her room to dash into the dinner dress Ethel had laid out for her.

To have her poverty-stricken home invaded by a host of strangers was striking a blow at the most sensitive weakness of this proud woman. And yet the loving motive which was so plain through it all, showing the very spirit in her dear children for which she had prayed, was too sacred a thing to be chilled by even a half-shade of disapproval.

"And who are coming, dear?" she asked of Meg, as soon as she could trust her voice.

"All the roomers, Momsy, excepting the little hunchback lady and Madame Coraline."

"Madame Coraline!" Mrs. Frey could not help exclaiming.

"Yes, Momsy. She accepted, and she *even came*, but she went back just now. She was dressed terribly fine—gold lace and green silk, but it was old and dowdy; and, Momsy, her cheeks were just as red! I was on the stepladder tackin' up the Bethlehem picture, Sisty was standin' on the high-chair hanging up the star, and Buddy's arms were full of gray moss that he was wrappin' round your chair. But we were just as polite to her as we could be, and asked her to take a seat. And we all thought she sat down; but she went, Momsy, and no one saw her go. Buddy says she's a witch. She left that flower-pot of sweet-basil on the table. I s'pose she brought it for a present. Do you think that we'd better send for her to come back, Momsy?"

"No, daughter, I think not. No doubt she had her own reasons for going, and she may come back. And are the rest all coming?"

"Yes'm; but we had a time gettin' Miss Guyosa to come. She says she's a First Family, an' she never mixes. But I told her so were we, and we mixed. And then I said that if she'd come she could sit at one end o' the table and carve the ham, while you'd do the turkey. But she says Buddy ought to do the turkey. But she's comin'. And, Momsy, the turkey is a perfect beauty. We put pecans in him. Miss Guyosa gave us the receipt and the nuts, too. Her cousin sent 'em to her from his plantation. And did you notice the paper roses in the moss festoons, Momsy? She made those. She has helped us fix up *a lot*. She made all the Easter flowers on St. Joseph's altar at the Cathedral, too, and—"

A rap at the door announcing a first guest sent the little cook bounding to the kitchen, while Ethel rushed into her mother's room, her mouth full of pins and her sash on her arm.

She had dressed the three little ones a half-hour ago; and Conrad, who had also made an early toilet, declared that they had all three walked round the dinner table thirty-nine times since their appearance in the "dining-room." When he advanced to do the honors, the small procession toddling single file behind him, somehow it had not occurred to him that he might encounter Miss Penny, the canary lady, standing in a dainty old dress of yellow silk just outside the door, nor, worse still, that she should bear in her hands a tiny cage containing a pair of young canaries.

He said afterwards that "everything would have passed off all right if it hadn't been for the twins." Of course he had forgotten that he had himself been the first one to compare Miss Penny to a canary.

By the time the little black-eyed woman had flitted into the door, and in a chirpy, bird-like voice wished them a merry Christmas, Felix had stuffed his entire handkerchief into his mouth. Was it any wonder that Félicie and Dorothea, seeing this, did actually disgrace the whole party by convulsions of laughter?

They were soon restored to order, though, by the little yellow-gowned lady herself, for it took but half a minute to say that the birds were a present for the twins—"the two little ones who brought me the invitation."

Such a present as this is no laughing matter, and, besides, the little Frey children were at heart polite. And so they had soon forgotten their mirth in their new joy.

And then other guests were presently coming in, and Mrs. Frey, looking startlingly fine and pretty in her fresh ruches and new tie, was saying pleasant things to everybody, while Ethel and Meg, tripping lightly in and out, brought in the dishes.

As there was no parlor, guests were received in the curtained end of the gallery. No one was disposed to be formal, and when the old Professor entered with a little brown-paper parcel, which he declared, after his greetings, to contain his dinner, everybody felt that the etiquette of the occasion was not to be very strict or in the least embarrassing.

Of course Mrs. Frey, as hostess, "hoped the Professor would reconsider, and have a slice of the Christmas turkey"; but when they had presently all taken their seats at the table, and the eccentric guest had actually opened his roll of bread and cheese upon his empty plate, over which he began to pass savory dishes to his neighbors, she politely let him have his way. Indeed, there was nothing else to do, as he declared—declining the first course with a wave of his hand—that he had come "yust for de sake of sociapility."

"I haf seen efery day doze children work und sing so nize togedder yust like leetle mans und ladies, so I come yust to eggsbress my t'anks for de compliment, und to make de acquaintance off doze nize y'ung neighbors." This with a courtly bow to each one of the children separately. And he added in a moment: "De dinner iss very fine, but for me one dinner iss yust like anudder. Doze are all externals."

To which measured and kindly speech Conrad could not help replying, "It won't be an external to us, Professor, by the time we get through."

"Oho!" exclaimed the old man, delighted with the boy's ready wit. "Dot's a wery schmart boy you got dhere, Mrs. Vrey."

At this exhibition of broken English the twins, who were waiting on the table, thought it safe to rush to the kitchen on pretence of changing plates, while Dorothea, seated at the Professor's left, found it necessary to bite both lips and to stare hard at the vinegar-cruet for fully a second to keep from laughing. Then, to make sure of her self-possession, she artfully changed the subject, remarking, dryly,

"My nickel buyed the ice."

This was much funnier than the Professor's speech, judging from the laughter that followed it. And Miss Dorothea Frey's manners were saved, which was the important thing.

It would be impossible in this short space to give a full account of this novel and interesting dinner party, but if any one supposes that there was a dull moment in it, he is altogether mistaken.

Mrs. Frey and Ethel saw to it that no one was neglected in conversation; Meg and Conrad looked after the prompt replenishing of plates, though the alert little waiters, Felix and Félicie, anticipated every want, and were as sprightly as two crickets, while Dorothea provoked frequent laughter by a random fire of unexpected remarks, never failing, for instance, to offer ice-water during every "still minute"; and, indeed, once that young lady did a thing that might have proved quite terrible had the old lady Saxony, who sat opposite, been disagreeable or sensitive.

What Dorothea said was innocent enough—only a single word of two letters, to begin with.

She had been looking blankly at her opposite neighbor for a full minute, when she suddenly exclaimed,

"Oh!"

That was all, but it made everybody look, first at Dolly and then across the table. Whereupon the little maid, seeing her blunder, hastened to add:

"That's nothin'. My grandma's come out too."

And then, of course, every one noticed that old lady Saxony held her dainty hemstitched handkerchief quite over her mouth. Fortunately Mrs. Saxony's good sense was as great as her appreciation of humor, and, as she shook her finger threateningly at Dorothea, her twinkling eyes gave everybody leave to laugh. So "Dolly's terrible break," as Conrad called it, really went far to making the dinner a success—that is, if story-telling and laughter and the merry clamor such as distinguish the gayest of dinner parties the world over count as success.

It was while the Professor was telling a funny story of his boy life in Germany that there came a rap at the door, and the children, thinking only of Madame

Coraline, turned their eyes towards the door, only to see the Italian organ-grinder, whom, in the excitement of the dinner party, they had forgotten to expect. He was to play for the children to dance after dinner, and had come a little early—or perhaps dinner was late.

Seeing the situation, the old man began bowing himself out, when the Professor, winking mysteriously at Mrs. Frey and gesticulating animatedly, pointed first to the old Italian and then to Madame Coraline's vacant chair. Everybody understood, and smiling faces had already shown approval when Mrs. Frey said, quietly, "Let's put it to vote. All in favor raise glasses."

THE ITALIAN ORGAN-GRINDER

Every glass went up. The old Italian understood little English, but the offer of a seat is a simple pantomime, and he was presently declining again and again, bowing lower each time, until before he knew it—all the time refusing—he was in the chair, his plate was filled, and Dolly was asking him to have ice-water. No guest of the day was more welcome. None enjoyed his dinner more, judging from the indications. And as to Meg, the moving spirit in the whole party, she was beside herself with delight over the unexpected guest.

The dinner all through was what Conrad called a "rattlin' success," and the evening afterwards, during which nearly every guest contributed some entertainment, was one long to be remembered. The Professor not only sang, but danced. Miss Penny whistled so like a canary that one could really believe her when she said she always trained her young birds' voices. Miss Guyosa told charming folk-lore anecdotes, handed down in her family since the old Spanish days in Louisiana.

The smiling organ-grinder played his engaged twenty-five cents' worth of tunes over and over again, and when the evening was done, persistently refused to take the money until Felix slipped it into his pocket.

The Frey party will long be remembered in the Coppenole house, and beyond it, too, for some very pleasant friendships date from this Christmas dinner. The old Professor was just the man to help Conrad with his German lessons. It was so easy for Meg to send him a cup of hot coffee on cold mornings. Mrs. Frey and Miss Guyosa soon found many ties in common friends of their youth. Indeed, the twins had gotten their French names from a remote creole cousin, who proved to be also a kinswoman to Miss Guyosa. It was such a comfort, when Mrs. Frey was kept out late at the office, for the children to have Miss Guyosa come and sit with them, telling stories or reading aloud; and they brought much brightness into her life too.

Madame Coraline soon moved away, and, indeed, before another Christmas the Freys had moved too—to a small cottage all their own, sitting in the midst of a pretty rose-garden. Here often come Miss Guyosa and the Professor, both welcome guests, and Conrad says the Professor makes love to Miss Guyosa, but it is hard to tell.

One cannot keep up with two people who can tell jokes in four languages, but the Professor has a way of dropping in as if by accident on the evenings Miss Guyosa is visiting the Freys, and they do read the same books—in four languages. There's really no telling.

When the Frey children are playing on the *banquette* at their front gate on sunny afternoons, the old organ-grinder often stops, plays a free tune or two for them to dance by, smilingly doffs his hat to the open window above, and passes on.

"THE PROFESSOR NOT ONLY SANG, BUT DANCED"

LITTLE MOTHER QUACKALINA

LITTLE MOTHER QUACKALINA
STORY OF A DUCK FARM
CHAPTER I

The black duck had a hard time of it from the beginning—that is, from the beginning of her life on the farm. She had been a free wild bird up to that time, swimming in the bay, playing hide-and-seek with her brothers and sisters and cousins among the marsh reeds along the bank, and coquettishly diving for "mummies" and catching them "on the swim" whenever she craved a fishy morsel. This put a fresh perfume on her breath, and made her utterly charming to her seventh cousin, Sir Sooty Drake, who always kept himself actually fragrant with the aroma of raw fish, and was in all respects a dashing beau. Indeed, she was behaving most coyly, daintily swimming in graceful curves around Sir Sooty among the marsh-mallow clumps at the mouth of "Tarrup Crik," when the shot was fired that changed all her prospects in life.

The farmer's boy was a hunter, and so had been his grandfather, and his grandfather's gun did its work with a terrific old-fashioned explosion.

When it shot into the great clump of pink mallows everything trembled. The air was full of smoke, and for a distance of a quarter of a mile away the toads crept out of their hiding and looked up and down the road. The chickens picking at the late raspberry bushes in the farmer's yard craned their necks, blinked, and didn't swallow another berry for fully ten seconds. And a beautiful green caterpillar, that had seen the great red rooster mark him with his evil eye, and expected to be gobbled up in a twinkling, had time to "hump himself" and crawl under a leaf before the astonished rooster recovered from the noise. This is a case where the firing of a gun saved at least one life. I wonder how many butterflies owe their lives to that gun?

As to the ducks in the clump of mallows that caught the volley, they simply tumbled over and gave themselves up for dead.

"THE FARMER'S BOY WAS A HUNTER"

The heroine of our little story, Lady Quackalina Blackwing, stayed in a dead faint for fully seventeen seconds, and the first thing she knew when she "came to" was that she was lying under the farmer boy's coat in an old basket, and that there was a terrific rumbling in her ears and a sharp pain in one wing, that something was sticking her, that Sir Sooty was nowhere in sight, and that she wanted her mother and all her relations.

Indeed, as she began to collect her senses, while she lay on top of the live crab that pinched her chest with his claw, she realized that there was not a cousin in the world, even to some she had rather disliked, that she would not have been most happy to greet at this trying moment.

The crab probably had no unfriendly intention. He was only putting up the best hand he had, trying to find some of his own kindred. He had himself been lying in a hole in shallow water when the farmer's boy raked him in and changed the whole course of his existence.

He and the duck knew each other by sight, but though they were both "in the swim," they belonged to different sets, and so were small comfort to one another on this journey to the farm.

They both knew some English, and as the farmer's boy spoke part English and part "farm," they understood him fairly well when he was telling the man digging potatoes in the field that he was going to "bile" the crab in a tomato can and to make a "decoy" out of the duck.

"Bile" and "decoy" were new words to the listeners in the basket, but they both knew about tomato cans. The bay and "Tarrup Crik" were strewn with them, and the crab had once hidden in one, half imbedded in the sand, when he was a "soft-shell." He knew their names, because he had studied them before their labels soaked off, and he knew there was no malice in them for him, though the young fishes who have soft outsides dreaded their sharp edges very much. There is sometimes some advantage in having one's skeleton on the surface, like a coat of mail.

And so the crab was rather pleased at the prospect of the tomato can. He thought the cans grew in the bay, and so he expected presently to be "biled" in his own home waters. The word "biled" probably meant *dropped in*. Ignorance is sometimes bliss, indeed.

Poor little Quackalina, however, was getting less comfort out of her ignorance. She thought "decoy" had a foreign sound, as if it might mean a French stew. She had had relations who had departed life by way of a *purée*, while others had gone into a *sauté* or *pâté*. Perhaps a "decoy" was a *pâté* with gravy or a *purée* with a crust on it. If worse came to the worst, she would prefer the *purée* with a crust. It would be more like decent burial.

Of course she thought these things in duck language, which is not put in here, because it is not generally understood. It is quite a different thing from Pidgin-English, and it isn't all "quack" any more than French is all "au revoir," or Turkey all "gobble, gobble," or goose only a string of "S's," or darkey all "howdy."

The crab's thoughts were expressed in his eyes, that began coming out like little telescopes until they stood quite over his cheeks. Maybe some people think crabs have no cheeks, but that isn't so. They have them, but they keep them inside, where they blush unseen, if they blush at all.

But this is the story of the black duck. However, perhaps some one who reads it will be pleased to know that the crab got away. He sidled up—sidled is a regular word in crab language—until his left eye could see straight into the boy's face, and then he waited. He had long ago found that there was nothing to be gained by pinching the duck. It only made a row in the basket and got him upset. But, by keeping very still and watching his chance, he managed to climb so near the top that when the basket gave a lurch he simply vaulted overboard and dropped in the field. Then he hid between three mushrooms and a stick until the boy's footsteps were out of hearing and he had time to draw in his eyes and start for the bay. He had lost his left claw some time before, and the new one he was growing was not yet very strong. Still, let us hope that he reached there in safety.

The duck knew when he had been trying to get out, but she didn't tell. She wanted him to go, for she didn't like his ways. Still, when he had gone, she felt lonely. Misery loves company—even though it be very poor company.

But Quackalina had not long to feel lonely. Almost any boy who has shot a duck walks home with it pretty fast, and this boy nearly ran. He would have run if his legs hadn't been so fat.

The first sound that Quackalina heard when they reached the gate was the quacking of a thousand ducks, and it frightened her so that she forgot all about the crab and her aching wing and even the decoy. The boy lived on a duck farm, and it was here that he had brought her. This would seem to be a most happy thing—but there are ducks and ducks. Poor little Quackalina knew the haughty quawk of the proud white ducks of Pekin. She knew that she would be only a poor colored person among them, and that she, whose mother and grandmother had lived in the swim of best beach circles and had looked down upon these incubator whitings, who were grown by the pound and had no relations whatever, would now have to suffer their scorn.

Even their distant quawk made her quake, though she feared her end was near. There are some trivial things that are irritating even in the presence of death.

But Quackalina was not soon to die. She did suffer some humiliations, and her wing was very painful, but a great discovery soon filled her with such joy that nothing else seemed worth thinking about.

There were three other black ducks on the farm, and they hastened to tell her that they were already decoys, and that the one pleasant thing in being a decoy was that it was *not* to be killed or cooked or eaten.

This was good news. The life of a decoy-duck was hard enough; but when one got accustomed to have its foot tied to the shore, and shots fired all around it, one grew almost to enjoy it. It was so exciting. But to the timid young duck who had never been through it it was a terrible prospect.

And so, for a long time, little Quackalina was a very sad duck. She loved her cousin, Sir Sooty, and she loved pink mallow blossoms. She liked to eat the "mummy" fish alive, and not cooked with sea-weed, as the farmer fed them to her.

But most of all she missed Sir Sooty. And so, two weeks later, when her wing was nearly well, in its new, drooping shape, what was her joy when he himself actually waddled into the farm-yard—into her very presence—without a single quack of warning.

The feathers of one of his beautiful wings were clipped, but he was otherwise looking quite well, and he hastened to tell her that he was happy, even in exile, to be with her again. And she believed him.

He had been captured in a very humiliating way, and this he made her promise never to tell. He had swum so near the decoy-duck that his foot had caught in its string, and before he could get away the farmer had him fast. "And now," he quacked, "I'm glad I did it," and Quackalina quacked, "So am I." And they were very happy.

"SIR SOOTY HIMSELF ACTUALLY WADDLED INTO THE FARM-YARD"

Indeed, they grew so blissful after a while that they decided to try to make the best of farm life and to settle down. So they began meandering about on long waddles—or waddling about on long meanders—all over the place, hunting for a cozy hiding-place for a nest. For five whole days they hunted before Quackalina finally settled down into the hollow that she declared was "just a fit" for her, under the edge of the old shanty where the Pekin feathers were stored.

White, fluffy feathers are very beautiful things, and they are soft and pleasant to our touch, but they are sad sights to ducks and geese, and Quackalina selected a place for her nest where she could never see the door open into this dread storehouse.

It was, indeed, very well hidden, and, as if to make it still more secure, a friendly golden-rod sprang up quite in front of it, and a growth of pepper-grass kindly closed in one side.

Quackalina had never been sent out on decoy duty, and after a time she ceased to fear it, but sometimes Sir Sooty had to go, and his little wife would feel very anxious until he came back.

There are some very sad parts in this little story, and we are coming to one of them now.

The home-nest had been made. There were ten beautiful eggs in it—all polished and shining like opals. And the early golden-rod that stood on guard before it was sending out a first yellow spray when troubles began to come.

CHAPTER II

Quackalina thought she had laid twice as many as ten eggs in the nest, but she could not be quite sure, and neither could Sir Sooty, though he thought so, too.

Very few poetic people are good at arithmetic, and even fine mathematicians are said to forget how to count when they are in love.

Certain it is, however, that when Quackalina finally decided to be satisfied to begin sitting, there were exactly ten eggs in the nest—just enough for her to cover well with her warm down and feathers.

"Sitting-time" may seem stupid to those who are not sitting; but Quackalina's breast was filled with a gentle content as she sat, day by day, behind the golden-rod, and blinked and reflected and listened for the dear "paddle, paddle" of Sir Sooty's feet, and his loving "qua', qua'"—a sort of caressing baby-talk that he had adopted in speaking to her ever since she had begun her long sitting.

"'I'M GOIN' TO SWAP 'EM'"

Quackalina was a patient little creature, and seldom left her nest, so that when she did so for a short walk in the glaring sun, she was apt to be dizzy and to see strange spots before her eyes. But this would all pass away when she got back to her cozy nest in the cool shade.

But one day it did not pass away—it got worse, or, at least, she thought it did. Instead of ten eggs in the nest she seemed to see twenty, and they were of a strange, dull color, and their shape seemed all wrong. She blinked her eyes nineteen times, and even rubbed them with her web-feet, so that she might not see double, but it was all in vain. Before her dazzled eyes twenty little pointed eggs lay, and when she sat upon them they felt strange to her breast. And then she grew faint and was too weak even to call Sir Sooty, but when he came waddling along presently, he found her so pale around the bill that he made her put out her tongue, and examined her symptoms generally.

Sir Sooty was not a regular doctor, but he was a very good quack, and she believed in him, which, in many cases, is the main thing.

So when he grew so tender that his words were almost like "qu, qu," and told her that she had been confined too closely and was threatened with *foie gras*, she only sighed and closed her eyes, and, keeping her fears to herself, hoped that the trouble was all in her eyes indeed—or her liver.

Now the sad part of this tale is that the trouble was not with poor little Quackalina's eyes at all. It was in the nest. The same farmer's boy who had kept her sitting of eggs down to ten by taking out one every day until poor Quackalina's patience was worn out—the same boy who had not used her as a decoy only because he wanted her to stay at home and raise little decoy-ducks—this boy it was who had now chosen to take her ten beautiful eggs and put them under a guinea-hen, and to fetch the setting of twenty guinea eggs for Quackalina to hatch out.

He did this just because, as he said, "That old black duck 'll hatch out as many eggs again as a guinea-hen will, an' the guinea 'll cover her ten eggs *easy*. I'm goin' to swap 'em." And "swap 'em" he did.

Nobody knows how the guinea-hen liked her sitting, for none but herself and the boy knew where her nest was hidden in a pile of old rubbish down by the cow-pond.

"MADE HER PUT OUT HER TONGUE"

When a night had passed, and a new day showed poor Quackalina the twenty little eggs actually under her breast—eggs so little that she could roll two at once under her foot—she did not know what to think. But like many patient people when great sorrows come, she kept very still and never told her fears.

She had never seen a guinea egg before in all her life. There were birds' nests in some of the reeds along shore, and she knew their little toy eggs. She knew the eggs of snakes, too, and of terrapins, or "tarrups," as they are called by the farmer folk along the bay.

When first she discovered the trouble in the nest she thought of these, and the very idea of a great procession of little turtles starting out from under her some fine morning startled her so that her head lay limp against the golden-rod for fully thirteen seconds. Then she got better, but it was not until she had taken a nip at the pepper-grass that she was sufficiently warmed up to hold up her head and think. And when she thought, she was comforted. These dainty pointed eggs were not in the least like the soft clumsy "double-enders" that the turtles lay in the sand. Besides, how could turtle-eggs have gotten there anyway? How much easier for one head to go wrong than twenty eggs.

She chuckled at the very folly of her fears, and nestling down into the place, she soon began to nod. And presently she had a funny, funny dream, which is much too long to go into this story, which is a great pity, for her dream is quite as interesting as the real story, although it is not half so true.

Sitting-time, after this, seemed very long to Quackalina, but after a while she began to know by various little stirrings under her downy breast that it was almost over. At the first real movement against her wing she felt as if everything about her was singing and saying, "mother! mother!" and bowing to her.

Even the pepper-grass nodded and the golden-rod, and careless roosters as they passed *seemed* to lower their combs to her and to forget themselves, just for a minute. And a great song was in her own bosom—a great song of joy—and although the sound that came from her beautiful coral bill was only a soft "qua', qua'," to common ears, to those who have the finest hearing it was full of a heavenly tenderness. But there was a tremor in it, too—a tremor of fear; and the fear was so terrible that it kept her from looking down even when she knew a little head was thrusting itself up through her great warm wing. She drew the wing as a caressing arm lovingly about it though, and saying to herself, "I must wait till they are all come; then I'll look," she gazed upward at the moon that was just showing a rim of gold over the hay-stack—and closed her eyes.

There was no sleep that long night for little mother Quackalina.

It was a great, great night. Under her breast, wonderful happenings every minute; outside, the white moonlight; and always in sight across the yard, just a dark object against the ground—Sir Sooty, sound asleep, like a philosopher!

Oh yes, it was a great, great night. Its last hours before day were very dark and sorrowful, and by the time a golden gleam shot out of the east Quackalina knew that her first glance into the nest must bring her grief. The tiny restless things beneath her brooding wings were chirping in an unknown tongue. But their wiry Japanesy voices, that clinked together like little copper kettles, were very young and helpless, and Quackalina was a true mother-duck, and her heart went out to them.

When the fatal moment came and she really looked down into the nest, her relief in seeing beautiful feathered things, at least, was greater than any other feeling. It was something not to have to mother a lot of "tarrups," certainly.

Little guineas are very beautiful, and when presently Quackalina found herself crossing the yard with her twenty dainty red-booted hatchlings, although she longed for her own dear, ugly, smoky, "beautiful" ducklings, she could not help feeling pleasure and pride in the exquisite little creatures that had stepped so briskly into life from beneath her own breast.

It was natural that she should have hurried to the pond with her brood. Wouldn't she have taken her own ducklings there? If these were only little "step-ducks," she was resolved that, in the language of step-mothers, "they should never know the difference." She would begin by taking them in swimming.

Besides, she longed for the pond herself. It was the place where she could best think quietly and get things straightened in her mind.

Sir Sooty had not seen her start off with her new family. He had said to himself that he had lost so much rest all night that he must have a good breakfast, and so, at the moment when Quackalina and the guineas slipped around the stable to the cow-pond, he was actually floundering in the very centre of one of the feed-troughs in the yard, and letting the farmer turn the great mass of cooked "feed" all over him. Greedy ducks often act that way. Even the snow-white Pekins do it. It is bad enough any time, but on the great morning when one becomes a papa-duck he ought to try to be dignified, and Sir Sooty knew it. And he knew full well that events had been happening all night in the nest, and that was why he said he had lost rest. But he hadn't. A great many people are like Sir Sooty. They say they lose sleep when they don't.

But listen to what was taking place at the cow-pond, for it is this that made this story seem worth the telling.

When Quackalina reached the pond, she flapped her tired wings three times from pure gladness at the sight of the beautiful water. And then, plunging in, she took one delightful dive before she turned to the shore, and in the sweetest tones invited the little ones to follow her.

But they—

Well, they just looked down at their red satin boots and shook their heads. And then it was that Quackalina noticed their feet, and saw that they would never swim.

It was a great shock to her. She paddled along shore quite near them for a while, trying to be resigned to it. And then she waddled out on the grassy bank, and fed them with some newts, and a tadpole, and a few blue-bottle flies, and a snail, and several other delicacies, which they seemed to enjoy quite as much as if they had been young ducks. And then Quackalina, seeing them quite happy, struck out for the very middle of the pond. She would have one glorious outing, at least. Oh, how sweet the water was! How it soothed the tender spots under her weary wings! How it cooled her ears and her tired eyelids! And now—and now—and now—as she dived and dipped and plunged—how it cheered and comforted her heart! How faithfully it bore her on its cool bosom! For a few minutes, in the simple joy of her bath, she even forgot to be sorrowful.

And now comes the dear part of the troublous tale of this little black mother-duck—the part that is so pleasant to write—the part that it will be good to read.

When at last Quackalina, turning, said to herself, "I must go ashore now and look after my little steppies," she raised her eyes and looked before her to see just where she was. And then the vision she seemed to see was so strange and so beautiful that—well, she said afterwards that she never knew just how she bore it.

Just before her, on the water, swimming easily on its trusty surface, were ten little ugly, smoky, "beautiful" ducks! Ten little ducks that looked precisely like every one of Quackalina's relations! And now they saw her and began swimming towards her.

Before she knew it, Quackalina had flapped her great wings and quacked aloud three times, and three times again! And she didn't know she was doing it, either.

She did know, though, that in less time than it has taken to tell it, her own ten beautiful ducks were close about her, and that she was kissing each one somewhere with her great red bill. And then she saw that upon the bank a nervous, hysterical guinea-hen was tearing along, and in a voice like a carving-knife screeching aloud with terror. It went through Quackalina's bosom like a neuralgia, but she didn't mind it very much. Indeed, she forgot it instantly when she looked down upon her ducklings again, and she even forgot to think about it any more. And so it was that the beautiful thing that was happening on the bank, under her very eyes almost, never came to Quackalina's knowledge at all.

When her own bosom was as full of joy as it could be, why should she have turned at the sound of the carving-knife voice to look ashore, and to notice that at its first note there were twenty little pocket-knife answers from over the pond, and that in a twinkling twenty pairs of red satin boots were running as fast as they could go to meet the great speckled mother-hen, whose blady voice was the sweetest music in all the world to them?

When, after quite a long time, Quackalina began to realize things, and thought of the little guineas, and said to herself, "Goodness gracious me!" she looked anxiously ashore for them, but not a red boot could she see. The whole delighted guinea family were at that moment having a happy time away off in the cornfield out of sight and hearing.

This was very startling, and Quackalina grieved a little because she couldn't grieve more. She didn't understand it at all, and it made her almost afraid to go ashore, so she kept her ten little ducklings out upon the water nearly all day.

And now comes a very amusing thing in this story.

When this great, eventful day was passed, and Quackalina was sitting happily among the reeds with her dear ones under her wings, while Sir Sooty waddled proudly around her with the waddle that Quackalina thought the most graceful walk in the world, she began to tell him what had happened, beginning at the time when she noticed that the eggs were wrong.

Sir Sooty listened very indulgently for a while, and then—it is a pity to tell it on him, but he actually burst out laughing, and told her, with the most patronizing quack in the world, that it was "all imagination."

"HER OWN TEN BEAUTIFUL DUCKS WERE CLOSE ABOUT HER"

And when Quackalina insisted with tears and even a sob or two that it was every word true, he quietly looked at her tongue again, and then he said a very long word for a quack doctor. It sounded like 'lucination. And he told Quackalina never, on any account, to tell any one else so absurd a tale, and that it was only a canard—which was very flippant and unkind, in several ways. There are times when even good jokes are out of place.

At this, Quackalina said that she would take him to the nest and show him the little pointed egg-shells. And she did take him there, too. Late at night, when all honest ducks, excepting somnambulists and such as have vindications on hand, are asleep, Quackalina led the way back to the old nest. But when she got there, although the clear, white moonlight lay upon everything and revealed every blade of grass, not a vestige of nest or straw or shell remained in sight.

The farmer's boy had cleared them all away.

By this time Quackalina began to be mystified herself, and after a while, seeing only her own ten ducks always near, and never sighting such a thing as little, flecked, red-booted guineas, she really came to doubt whether it had all happened or not.

And even to this day she is not quite sure. How she and all her family finally got away and became happy wild birds again is another story. But while Quackalina sits and blinks upon the bank among the mallows, with all her ugly "beautiful" children around her, she sometimes even yet wonders if the whole thing could have been a nightmare, after all.

But it was no nightmare. It was every word true. If anybody doesn't believe it, let him ask the guineas.

OLD EASTER

OLD EASTER

Nearly everybody in New Orleans knew Old Easter, the candy-woman. She was very black, very wrinkled, and very thin, and she spoke with a wiry, cracked voice that would have been pitiful to hear had it not been so merry and so constantly heard in the funny high laughter that often announced her before she turned a street corner, as she hobbled along by herself with her old candy-basket balanced on her head.

People who had known her for years said that she had carried her basket in this way for so long that she could walk more comfortably with it than without it. Certainly her head and its burden seemed to give her less trouble than her feet, as she picked her way along the uneven *banquettes* with her stick. But then her feet were tied up in so many rags that even if they had been young and strong it would have been hard for her to walk well with them. Sometimes the rags were worn inside her shoes and sometimes outside, according to the shoes she wore. All of these were begged or picked out of trash heaps, and she was not at all particular about them, just so they were big enough to hold her old rheumatic feet—though she showed a special liking for men's boots.

When asked why she preferred to wear boots she would always answer, promptly, "Ter keep off snake bites"; and then she would almost certainly, if there were listeners enough, continue in this fashion: "You all young trash forgits dat I dates back ter de snake days in dis town. Why, when I was a li'l' gal, about *so* high, I was walkin' along Canal Street one day, barefeeted, an' not lookin' down, an' terrectly I feel some'h'n' nip me '*snip!*' in de big toe, an' lookin' quick I see a grea' big rattlesnake—"

As she said "snip," the street children who were gathered around her would start and look about them, half expecting to see a great snake suddenly appear upon the flag-stones of the pavement.

OLD EASTER

At this the old woman would scream with laughter as she assured them that there were thousands of serpents there now that they couldn't see, because they had only "single sight," and that many times when they thought mosquitoes were biting them they were being "'tackted by deze heah onvisible snakes."

It is easy to see why the children would gather about her to listen to her talk.

Nobody knew how old Easter was. Indeed, she did not know herself, and when any one asked her, she would say, "I 'spec' I mus' be 'long about twenty-fo'," or, "Don't you reckon I mus' be purty nigh on to nineteen?" And then, when she saw from her questioner's face that she had made a mistake, she would add, quickly:

"I means twenty-fo' *hund'ed*, honey," or, "I means a *hund'ed* an' nineteen," which latter amendment no doubt came nearer the truth.

Having arrived at a figure that seemed to be acceptable, she would generally repeat it, in this way:

"Yas, missy; I was twenty-fo' hund'ed years ole las' Easter Sunday."

The old woman had never forgotten that she had been named Easter because she was born on that day, and so she always claimed Easter Sunday as her birthday, and no amount of explanation would convince her that this was not always true.

"What diff'ence do it make ter me ef it comes soon or late, I like ter know?" she would argue. "Ef it comes soon, I gits my birfday presents dat much quicker; an' ef it comes late, you all got dat much mo' time ter buy me some mo'. 'Tain't fur me ter deny my birfday caze it moves round."

And then she would add, with a peal of her high, cracked laughter: "Seem ter me, de way I keeps a-livin' on—an' a-livin' on—*an' a-livin' on*—maybe deze heah slip-aroun' birfdays don't pin a pusson down ter ole age so close't as de clock-work reg'lars does."

And then, if she were in the mood for it, she would set her basket down, and, without lifting her feet from the ground, go through a number of quick and comical movements, posing with her arms and body in a way that was absurdly like dancing.

Old Easter had been a very clever woman in her day, and many an extra picayune had been dropped into her wrinkled palm—nobody remembered the time when it wasn't wrinkled—in the old days, just because of some witty answer she had given while she untied the corner of her handkerchief for the coins to make change in selling her candy.

"'YAS, MISSY, I WAS TWENTY FO' HOND'ED YEARS OLE, LAS' EASTER SUNDAY'"

One of the very interesting things about the old woman was her memory. It was really very pleasant to talk with a person who could distinctly recall General Jackson and Governor Claiborne, who would tell blood-curdling tales of Lafitte the pirate and of her own wonderful experiences when as a young girl she had served his table at Barataria.

If, as her memory failed her, the old creature was tempted into making up stories to supply the growing demand, it would not be fair to blame her too severely. Indeed, it is not at all certain that, as the years passed, she herself knew which of the marvellous tales she related were true and which made to order.

"Yas, sir," she would say, "I ricollec' when all dis heah town wasn't nothin' but a alligator swamp—no houses—no fences—no streets—no gas-postes—no 'lection lights—no—*no river—no nothin'*!"

If she had only stopped before she got to the river, she would have kept the faith of her hearers better, but it wouldn't have been half so funny.

"There wasn't anything here then but you and the snakes, I suppose?" So a boy answered her one day, thinking to tease her a little.

"Yas, me an' de snakes an' alligators an' Gineral Jackson an' my ole marster's gran'daddy an'—"

"And Adam?" added the mischievous fellow, still determined to worry her if possible.

"Yas, Marse Adam an' ole Mistus, Mis' Eve, an' de great big p'isonous fork-tailed snake wha' snatch de apple dat Marse Adam an' Mis' Eve was squabblin' over—an' et it up!"

When she had gotten this far, while the children chuckled, she began reaching for her basket, that she had set down upon the *banquette*. Lifting it to her head, now, she walled her eyes around mysteriously as she added:

"Yas, an' you better look out fur dat p'isonous fork-tailed snake, caze he's agoin' roun' hear right now; an' de favoristest dinner dat he craves ter eat is des sech no-'count, sassy, questionin' street-boys like you is."

And with a toss of her head that set her candy-basket swaying and a peal of saw-teeth laughter, she started off, while her would-be teaser found that the laugh was turned on himself.

It was sometimes hard to know when Easter was serious or when she was amusing herself—when she was sensible or when she wandered in her mind. And to the thoughtless it was always hard to take her seriously.

Only those who, through all her miserable rags and absurdities, saw the very poor and pitiful old, old woman, who seemed always to be companionless and alone, would sometimes wonder about her, and, saying a kind and encouraging word, drop a few coins in her slim, black hand without making her lower her basket. Or they would invite her to "call at the house" for some old worn flannels or odds and ends of cold victuals.

And there were a few who never forgot her in their Easter offerings, for which, as for all other gifts, she was requested to "call at the back gate." This seemed, indeed, the only way of reaching the weird old creature, who had for so many years appeared daily upon the streets, nobody seemed to know from where, disappearing with the going down of the sun as mysteriously as the golden disk itself. Of course, if any one had cared to insist upon knowing how she lived or where she stayed at nights, he might have followed her at a distance. But it is sometimes very easy for a very insignificant and needy person to rebuff those who honestly believe themselves eager to help. And so, when Old Easter, the candy-woman, would say, in answer to inquiries about her life, "I sleeps at night 'way out by de Metarie Ridge Cemetery, an' gets up in de mornin' up at de Red Church. I combs my ha'r wid de *latanier*, an' washes my face in de Ole Basin," it was so easy for those who wanted to help her to say to their consciences, "She doesn't want us to know where she lives," and, after a few simple kindnesses, to let the matter drop.

The above ready reply to what she would have called their "searchin' question" proved her a woman of quick wit and fine imagination. Anybody who knows New Orleans at all well knows that Metarie Ridge Cemetery, situated out of town in the direction of the lake shore, and the old Red Church, by the riverside above Carrollton, are several miles apart. People know this as well as they know that the *latanier* is the palmetto palm of the Southern wood, with its comb-like, many-toothed leaves, and that the Old Basin is a great pool of scum-covered, murky water, lying in a thickly-settled part of the French town, where numbers of small sailboats, coming in through the bayou with their cargoes of lumber from the coast of the Sound, lie against one another as they discharge and receive their freight.

If all the good people who knew her in her grotesque and pitiful street character had been asked suddenly to name the very poorest and most miserable person in New Orleans, they would almost without doubt have immediately replied, "Why, old Aunt Easter, the candy-woman. Who could be poorer than she?"

To be old and black and withered and a beggar, with nothing to recommend her but herself—her poor, insignificant, ragged self—who knew nobody and whom nobody knew—that was to be poor, indeed.

Of course, Old Easter was not a professional beggar, but it was well known that before she disappeared from the streets every evening one end of her long candy-basket was generally pretty well filled with loose paper parcels of cold victuals, which she was always sure to get at certain kitchen doors from kindly people who didn't care for her poor brown twists. There had been days in the past when Easter peddled light, porous sticks of snow-white taffy, cakes of toothsome sugar-candy filled with fresh orange-blossoms, and pralines of pecans or cocoa-nut. But one cannot do everything.

One cannot be expected to remember General Jackson, spin long, imaginative yarns of forgotten days, and make up-to-date pralines at the same time. If the people who had ears to listen had known the thing to value, this old, old woman could have sold her memories, her wit, and even her imagination better than she had ever sold her old-fashioned sweets.

But the world likes molasses candy. And so Old Easter, whose meagre confections grew poorer as her stories waxed in richness, walked the streets in rags and dirt and absolute obscurity.

An old lame dog, seeming instinctively to know her as his companion in misery, one day was observed to crouch beside her, and, seeing him, she took down her basket and entertained him from her loose paper parcels.

And once—but this was many years ago, and the incident was quite forgotten now—when a crowd of street fellows began pelting Crazy Jake, a foolish, half-paralyzed black boy, who begged along the streets, Easter had stepped before him, and, after receiving a few of their clods in her face, had struck out into the gang of his tormenters, grabbed two of its principal leaders by the seats of their trousers, spanked them until they begged for mercy, and let them go.

Nobody knew what had become of Crazy Jake after that. Nobody cared. The poor human creature who is not due at any particular place at any particular time can hardly be missed, even when the time comes when he himself misses the *here* and the *there* where he has been wont to spend his miserable days, even when he, perhaps having no one else, it is possible that he misses his tormenters.

It was a little school-girl who saw the old woman lower her basket to share her scraps with the street dog. It seemed to her a pretty act, and so she told it when she went home. And she told it again at the next meeting of the particular "ten" of the King's Daughters of which she was a member.

And this was how the name of Easter, the old black candy-woman, came to be written upon their little book as their chosen object of charity for the coming year.

The name was not written, however, without some opposition, some discussion, and considerable argument. There were several of the ten who could not easily consent to give up the idea of sending their little moneys to an Indian or a Chinaman—or to a naked black fellow in his native Africa.

There is something attractive in the savage who sticks bright feathers in his hair, carries a tomahawk, and wears moccasins upon his nimble feet. Most young people take readily to the idea of educating a picturesque savage and teaching him that the cast-off clothes they send him are better than his beads and feathers. The picturesque quality is very winning, find it where we may.

People at a distance may see how very much more interesting and picturesque the old black woman, Easter, was than any of these, but she did not seem so to the ten good little maidens who finally agreed to adopt her for their own—to find her out in her home life, and to help her.

With them it was an act of simple pity—an act so pure in its motive that it became in itself beautiful.

Perhaps the idea gained a little following from the fact that Easter Sunday was approaching, and there was a pleasing fitness in the old woman's name when it was proposed as an object for their Easter offerings. But this is a slight consideration.

Certainly when three certain very pious little maidens started out on the following Saturday morning to find the old woman, Easter, they were full of interest in their new object, and chattered like magpies, all three together, about the beautiful things they were going to do for her.

Somehow, it never occurred to them that they might not find her either at the Jackson Street and St. Charles Avenue corner, or down near Lee Circle, or at the door of the Southern Athletic Club, at the corner of Washington and Prytania streets.

But they found her at none of the familiar haunts; they did not discover any trace of her all that day, or for quite a week afterward. They had inquired of the grocery-man at the corner where she often rested—of the portresses of several schools where she sometimes peddled her candy at recess-time, and at the bakery where she occasionally bought a loaf of yesterday's bread. But nobody remembered having seen her recently.

Several people knew and were pleased to tell how she always started out in the direction of the swamp every evening when the gas was lit in the city, and that she turned out over the bridge along Melpomene Street, stopping to collect stray bits of cabbage leaves and refuse vegetables where the bridgeway leads through

Dryades Market. Some said that she had a friend there, who hid such things for her to find, under one of the stalls, but this may not have been true.

It was on the Saturday morning after their first search that three little "Daughters of the King" started out a second time, determined if possible to trace Old Easter to her hiding-place.

It was a shabby, ugly, and crowded part of town in which, following the bridged road, and inquiring as they went, they soon found themselves.

For a long time it seemed a fruitless search, and they were almost discouraged when across a field, limping along before a half-shabby, fallen gate, they saw an old, lame, yellow dog.

It was the story of her sharing her dinner with the dog on the street that had won these eager friends for the old woman, and so, perhaps, from an association of ideas, they crossed the field, timidly, half afraid of the poor miserable beast that at once attracted and repelled them.

But they need not have feared. As soon as he knew they were visitors, the social fellow began wagging his little stump of a tail, and with a sort of coaxing half-bark asked them to come in and make themselves at home.

Not so cordial, however, was the shy and reluctant greeting of the old woman, Easter, who, after trying in vain to rise from her chair as they entered her little room, motioned to them to be seated on her bed. There was no other seat vacant, the second chair of the house being in use by a crippled black man, who sat out upon the back porch, nodding.

As they took their seats, the yellow dog, who had acted as usher, squatted serenely in their midst, with what seemed a broad grin upon his face, and then it was that the little maid who had seen the incident recognized him as the poor old street dog who had shared old Easter's dinner.

Two other dogs, poor, ugly, common fellows, had strolled out as they came in, and there were several cats lying huddled together in the sun beside the chair of the sleeping figure on the back porch.

It was a poor little home—as poor as any imagination could picture it. There were holes in the floor—holes in the roof—cracks everywhere. It was, indeed, not considered, to use a technical word, "tenable," and there was no rent to pay for living in it.

But, considering things, it was pretty clean. And when its mistress presently recovered from her surprise at her unexpected visitors, she began to explain that "ef she'd 'a' knowed dey was comin' to call, she would 'a' scoured up a little."

Her chief apologies, however, were for the house itself and its location, "away outside o' quality neighborhoods in de swampy fields."

"I des camps out here, missy," she finally explained, "bec'ase dey's mo' room an' space fur my family." And here she laughed—a high, cracked peal of laughter—as she waved her hand in the direction of the back porch.

"Dey ain't nobody ter pleg Crazy Jake out here, an' him an' me, wid deze here lame an' crippled cats an' dogs—why, we sets out yonder an' talks together in de evenin's after de 'lection lights is lit in de tower market and de moon is lit in de sky. An' Crazy Jake—why, when de moon's on de full, Crazy Jake he can talk knowledge good ez you kin. I fetched him out here about a million years ago, time dey was puttin' him in de streets, caze dey was gwine hurt him. An' he knows mighty smart, git him ter talkin' right time o' de moon! But mos' gin'ally he forgits.

"Ef I hadn't 'a' fell an' sprained my leg las' week, de bread it wouldn't 'a' 'mos' give out, like it is, but I done melt down de insides o' some ole condense'-milk cans, an' soak de dry bread in it for him, an' to-morrer I'm gwine out ag'in. Yas, to-morrer I'm bleeged to go, caze you know to-morrer dats my birfday, an' all my family dey looks for a party on my birfday—don't you, you yaller, stub-tail feller you! Ef e warn't sort o' hongry, I'd make him talk fur yer; but I 'ain't learnt him much yit. He's my new-comer!"

This last was addressed to the yellow dog.

"'DE CATS? WHY, HONEY, DEY WELCOME TO COME AN' GO'"

"I had blin' Pete out here till 'istiddy. I done 'dopted him las' year, but he struck out ag'in beggin', 'caze he say he can't stand dis heah soaked victuals. But Pete, he ain't rale blin', nohow. He's des got a sinkin' sperit, an' he can't work, an' I keeps him caze a sinkin' sperit what ain't got no git-up to it hit's a heap wuss 'n blin'ness. He's got deze heah yaller-whited eyes, an' when he draps his leds over 'em an' trimbles 'em, you'd swear he was stone-blin', an' dat stuff wha' he rubs on 'em it's inju'ious to de sight, so I keeps him and takes keer of him now so I won't have a blin' man on my hands—an' to save him f'om sin, too.

"Ma'am? What you say, missy? De cats? Why, honey, dey welcome to come an' go. I des picked 'em up here an' dar 'caze dey was whinin'. Any breathin' thing dat I sees dat's poorer 'n what I is, why, I fetches 'em out once-t, an' dey mos' gin'ally stays.

"But if you yo'ng ladies 'll come out d'reckly after Easter Sunday, when I got my pervisions in, why I'll show you how de ladies intertain dey company in de old days when Gin'ral Jackson used ter po' de wine."

Needless to say, there was such a birthday party as had never before been known in the little shanty on the Easter following the visit of the three little maids of the King's Daughters.

When Old Easter had finished her duties as hostess, sharing her good things equally with those who sat at her little table and those who squatted in an outer circle on the floor, she remarked that it carried her away back to old times when she stood behind the governor's chair "while he h'isted his wineglass an' drink ter de ladies' side curls." And Crazy Jake said yes, he remembered, too. And then he began to nod, while blind Pete remarked, "To my eyes de purtiest thing about de whole birfday party is de bo'quet o' Easter lilies in de middle o' de table."

SAINT IDYL'S LIGHT

SAINT IDYL'S LIGHT

You would never have guessed that her name was Idyl—the slender, angular little girl of thirteen years who stood in her faded gown of checkered homespun on the brow of the Mississippi River. And fancy a saint balancing a bucket of water on top of her head!

Yet, as she puts the pail down beside her, the evening sun gleaming through her fair hair seems to transform it into a halo, as some one speaks her name, "Saint Idyl."

Her thin, little ears, sun-filled as she stands, are crimson disks; and the outlines of her upper arms, dimly seen through the flimsy sleeves, are as meagre as are the ankles above her bare, slim feet.

The appellation "Saint Idyl," given first in playful derision, might have been long ago forgotten but for the incident which this story records.

It was three years before, when the plantation children, colored and white together, had been saying, as is a fashion with them, what they would like to be.

One had chosen a "blue-eyed lady wid flounces and a pink fan," another a "fine white 'oman wid long black curls an' ear-rings," and a third would have been "a hoop-skirted lady wid a tall hat."

It was then that Idyl, the only white child of the group—the adopted orphan of the overseer's family—had said:

"I'd choose to be a saint, like the one in the glass winder in the church, with light shinin' from my head. I'd walk all night up and down the 'road bend,' so travellers could see the way and wagons wouldn't get stallded."

The children had shuddered and felt half afraid at this.

"But you'd git stallded yo'se'f in dat black mud—"

"An' de runaways in de canebrake 'd ketch yer—"

"An' de paterole'd shoot yer—"

"An' eve'body'd think you was a walkin' sperit, an' run away f'om yer."

So the protests had come in, though the gleaming eyes of the little negroes had shown their delight in the fantastic idea.

"But I'd walk on a cloud, like the saint in the picture," Idyl had insisted. "And my feet wouldn't touch the mud, and when the runaways looked into my face, they'd try to be good and go back to their masters. Nobody would hurt me. Tired horses would be glad to see my light, and everybody would love me."

So, first laughingly, and then as a matter of habit, she had come to be known as "Saint Idyl."

As she stands quite still, with face uplifted, out on the levee this evening, one is reminded in looking at her of the "Maid of Domremi" listening to the voices.

Idyl was in truth listening to voices—voices new, strange, and solemn—voices of heavy, distant cannon.

It was the 23d of April, 1862. A few miles below Bijou Plantation Farragut's fleet was storming the blockade at Fort Jackson. All along the lower Mississippi it was a time of dread and terror.

The negroes, for the most part awed and terror-stricken, muttered prayers as they went about, and all night long sang mournfully and shouted and prayed in the churches or in groups in their cabins, or even in the road.

The war had come at last. Its glare was upon the sky at night, and all day long reiterated its persistent staccato menace:

"Boom-m-m! Gloom-m-m! Tomb-b-b! Doom-m-m!"

The air had never seemed to lose the vibratory tremor, "M-m-m!" since the first gun, nearly six days ago.

It was as if the lips of the land were trembling. And the trembling lips of the black mothers, as they pressed their babes to their bosoms, echoed the wordless terror.

Death was in the air. Had they doubted it? In a field near by a shell had fallen, burying itself in the earth, and, exploding, had sent two men into the air, killing one and returning the other unhurt.

Now the survivor, saved as by a miracle, was preaching "The Wrath to Come."

To quote from himself, he had "been up to heaven long enough to get 'ligion." He had "gone up a lost sinner and come down a saved soul. Bless Gord!"

Regarding his life as charmed, the blacks followed him in crowds, while he descanted upon the text: "Then two shall be in the field. One shall be taken and the other left."

A great revival was in progress.

But this afternoon the levee at Bijou had been the scene of a new panic.

Rumor said that the blockade chain had been cut. Farragut's war monsters might any moment come snorting up the river. Nor was this all. The only local defence here was a volunteer artillery company of "Exempts." Old "Captain Doc," their leader, also local druggist and postmaster (doctor and minister only in emergency), was a unique and picturesque figure. Full of bombast as of ultimate kindness of feeling, he was equally happy in all of his four offices.

The "Rev. Capt. Doc, M.D.," as he was wont, on occasion, to call himself—why drag in a personal name among titles in themselves sufficiently distinguishing?—was by common consent the leading man with a certain underpopulation along the coast. And when, three months before, he had harangued them as to the patriot's duty of home defence, there was not a worthy incapable present but enthusiastically enlisted.

The tension of the times forbade perception of the ludicrous. For three months the "Riffraffs"—so they proudly called themselves—rheumatic, deaf, palsied, halt, lame, and one or two nearly blind, had represented "the cause," "the standing army," "le grand militaire," to the inflammable imaginations of this handful of simple rural people of the lower coast.

Of the nine "odds and ends of old cannon" which Captain Doc had been able to collect, it was said that but one would carry a ball. Certainly, of the remaining seven, one was of wood, an ancient gunsmith's sign, and another a gilded papier-mâché affair of a former Mystick Krewe.

Still, these answered for drill purposes, and would be replaced by genuine guns when possible. They were quite as good for everything excepting a battle, and in that case, of course, it would be a simple thing "to seize the enemy's guns" and use them.

When the Riffraffs had paraded up and down the river road no one had smiled, and if anybody realized that their captain wore the gorgeous pompon of a drum-major, its fitness was not questioned.

It was becoming to him. It corresponded to his lordly strut, and was in keeping with the stentorian tones that shouted "Halt!" or "Avance!"

Captain Doc appealed to Americans and creoles alike, and the Riffraffs marched quite as often to the stirring measures of "La Marseillaise" as to "The Bonny Blue Flag."

Ever since the first guns at the forts, the good captain had been disporting himself in full feather. He was "ready for the enemy."

His was a pleasing figure, and even inspiring as a picturesque embodiment of patriotic zeal; but when this afternoon the Riffraffs had planted their artillery along the levee front, while the little captain rallied them to "prepare to die by their guns," it was a different matter.

The company, loyal to a man, had responded with a shout, the blacksmith, to whose deaf ears his anvil had been silent for twenty years, throwing up his hat with the rest, while the epileptic who manned the papier-mâché gun was observed to scream the loudest.

Suddenly a woman, catching the peril of the situation, shrieked:

"They're going to fire on the gunboats! We'll all be killed."

Another caught the cry, and another. A mad panic ensued; women with babies in their arms gathered about Captain Doc, entreating him, with tears and cries, to desist.

But for once the tender old man, whose old boast had been that one tear from a woman's eyes "tore his heart open," was deaf to all entreaty.

The Riffraffs represented an injured faction. They had not been asked to enlist with the "Coast Defenders"—since gone into active service—and they seemed intoxicated by the present opportunity to "show the stuff they were made of."

At nearly nightfall the women, despairing and wailing, had gone home. Amid all the excitement the little girl Idyl had stood apart, silent. No one had noticed her, nor that, when all the others had gone, she still lingered.

Even Mrs. Magwire, the overseer's wife, with whom she lived, had forgotten to hurry or to scold her. What emotions were surging in her young bosom no one could know.

There was something in the cannon's roar that charmed her ear—something suggestive of strength and courage. Within her memory she had known only weakness and fear.

After the yellow scourge of '53, when she was but four years old, she had realized vaguely that strange people with loud voices and red faces had come to be to her in the place of father and mother, that the Magwire babies were heavy to carry, and that their mother had but a poor opinion of a "lazy hulk av a girrl that could not heft a washtub without panting."

Idyl had tried hard to be strong and to please her foster-mother, but there was, somehow, in her life at the Magwires' something that made her great far-away eyes grow larger and her poor little wrists more weak and slender.

She envied the Magwire twins—with all their prickly heat and their calico-blue eyes—when their mother pressed them lovingly to her bosom. She even envied the black babies when their great black mammies crooned them to sleep.

What does it matter, black or white or red, if one is loved?

An embroidered "Darling" upon an old crib-blanket, and a daguerreotype—a slender youth beside a pale, girlish woman, who clasped a big-eyed babe—these were her only tokens of past affection.

There was something within her that responded to the daintiness of the loving stitches in the old blanket—and to a something in the refined faces in the picture. And they had called their wee daughter "Idyl"—a little poem.

Yet she, not understanding, hated this name because of Mrs. Magwire, whose most merciless taunt was, "Sure ye're well named, ye idle dthreamer."

Mrs. Magwire, a well-meaning woman withal, measured her maternal kindnesses to the hungry-hearted orphan beneath her roof in generous bowls of milk and hunks of corn-bread.

Idyl's dreams of propitiating her were all of abstractions—self-sacrifice, patience, gratitude.

And she was as unconscious as was her material benefactress that she was an idealist, and why the combination resulted in inharmony.

This evening, as she stood alone upon the levee, listening to the cannon, a sudden sense of utter desolation and loneliness came to her. She only of all the plantation was unloved—forgotten—in this hour of danger.

A desperate longing seized her as she turned and looked back upon the nest of cabins. If she could only save the plantation! For love, no sacrifice could be too great.

With the thought came an inspiration. There was reason in the women's fears. Should the Riffraffs fire upon the fleet, surely guns would answer, else what was war?

She glanced at her full pail, and then at the row of cannon beside her.

If she could pour water into them! It was too light yet, but to-night—

How great and daring a deed to come to tempt the mind of a timid, delicate child who had never dared anything—even Mrs. Magwire's displeasure!

All during the evening, while Mother Magwire rocked the babies, moaning and weeping, Idyl, wiping her dishes in the little kitchen, would step to the door and peer out at the levee where the guns were. Every distant cannon's roar seemed to challenge her to the deed.

When finally her work was done, she slipped noiselessly out and started towards the levee, pail in hand; but as she approached it she saw moving shadows.

The Riffraffs were working at the guns. Seeing her project impossible, she sat down in a dark shadow by the roadside—studied the moving figures—listened to the guns which came nearer as the hours passed.

It was long after midnight; accelerated firing was proclaiming a crisis in the battle, when, suddenly, there came the rattle of approaching wheels accompanied by a noisy rabble. Then a woman screamed.

Captain Doc was coming with a wagon-load of ammunition. The guns were to be loaded.

The moon, a faint waning crescent, faded to a filmy line as a pillar of fire, rising against the sky northward towards the city, exceeded the glare of the battle below.

The darkness was quite lifted now, up and down the levee, and Idyl, standing in the shadow, could see groups of people weeping, wringing their hands, as Captain Doc, pompon triumphant, came in sight galloping down the road.

In a second more he would pass the spot where she stood—stood unseen, seeing the sorrow of the people, heeding the challenge of the guns. The wagon was at hand.

With a faint, childish scream, raising her thin arms heavenward, she plunged forward and fell headlong in its path.

The victory was hers.

The tinselled captain was now tender surgeon, doctor, friend.

In his own arms he raised the limp little form from beneath the wheel, while the shabby gray coats of a dozen "Riffraffs," laid over the cannon-balls in the wagon, made her a hero's bed; and Captain Doc, seizing the reins, turned the horses cautiously, and drove in haste back to his drug-store.

Farragut's fleet and "the honor of the Riffraffs" were forgotten in the presence of this frail embodiment of death.

Upon his own bed beside an open window he laid her, and while his eager company became surgeon's assistants, he tenderly bound her wounds.

For several hours she lay in a stupor, and when she opened her eyes the captain knelt beside her. Mrs. Magwire stood near, noisily weeping.

"Is it saved?" she asked, when at length she opened her eyes.

Captain Doc, thinking her mind was wandering, raised her head, and pointed to the river, now ablaze with light.

"See," said he. "See the steamboats loaded with burning cotton, and the great ship meeting them; that is a Yankee gunboat! See, it is passing."

"And you didn't shoot? And are the people glad?"

"No, we didn't shoot. You fell and got hurt at the dark turn by the acacia bushes, where you hang your little lantern on dark nights. Some one ought to have hung one for you to-night. How did it happen, child?"

"It didn't happen. I did it on purpose. I knew if I got hurt you would stop and cure me, and not fire at the boats. I wanted to save—to save the plan—"

While the little old man raised a glass to the child's lips his hand shook, and something like a sob escaped him.

"Listen, little one," he whispered, while his lips quivered. "I am an old fool, but not a fiend—not a devil. Not a gun would have fired. I wet all the powder. I didn't want anybody to say the Riffraffs flinched at the last minute. But you—oh, my God!" His voice sank even lower. "You have given your young life for my folly."

She understood.

"I haven't got any pain—only—I can't move. I thought I'd get hurt worse than I am—and not so much. I feel as if I were going up—and up—through the red—into the blue. And the moon is coming sideways to me. And her face—it is in it—just like the picture." She cast her eyes about the room as if half conscious of her surroundings. "Will they—will they love me now?"

Mrs. Magwire, sobbing aloud, fell upon her knees beside the bed.

"God love her, the heavenly child!" she wailed. "She was niver intinded for this worrld. Sure, an' I love ye, darlint, jist the same as Mary Ann an' Kitty—an' betther, too, to make up the loss of yer own mother, God rest her."

Great tears rolled down the cheeks of the dying child, and that heavenly light which seems a forecast of things unseen shone from her brilliant eyes.

She laid her thin hand upon Mrs. Magwire's head, buried now upon the bed beside her.

"Lay the little blanket on me, please—when I go—"

She turned her eyes upon the sky.

"She worked it for me—the 'Darling' on it. The moon is coming again—sideways. It is her face."

So, through the red of the fiery sky, up into the blue, passed the pure spirit of little Saint Idyl.

The river seemed afire now with floating chariots of flame.

Slowly, majestically, upward into this fiery sea rode the fleet.

Although many of the negroes had run frightened into the woods, the conflagration revealed an almost unbroken line on either side of the river, watching the spectacular pageant with awe-stricken, ashy faces.

At Bijou a line of men—not the Riffraffs—sat astride the cannon, over the mouths of which they hung their hats or coats.

"I tell yer deze heah Yankees mus' be monst'ous-sized men. Look at de big eye-holes 'longside o' de ship," said one—a young black fellow.

"Eye-holes!" retorted an old man sitting apart; "dem ain't no eye-holes, chillen. Dey gun-holes! Dat what dey is! An' ef you don't keep yo' faces straight dey'll 'splode out on you 'fo' you know it."

The first speaker rolled backward down the levee, half a dozen following. The old man sat unmoved. Presently a little woolly head peered over the bank.

"What de name o' dat fust man-o'-war, gran'dad?"

"Name *Freedom*." The old man answered without moving. "Freedom comin' wid guns in 'er mouf, ready to spit fire, I tell yer!"

"Jeems, heah, say all de no-'count niggers is gwine be sol' over ag'in—is dat so, gran'dad?"

"Yas; every feller gwine be sol' ter 'isself. An' a mighty onery, low-down marster heap ob 'em 'll git, too."

It was nearly day when Captain Doc, pale and haggard, joined the crowd upon the levee.

As he stepped upon its brow, a woman, fearing the provocation of his military hat, begged him to remove it.

It might provoke a volley.

Raising the hat, the captain turned and solemnly addressed the crowd:

"My countrymen," he began, and his voice trembled, "the Riffraffs are disbanded. See!"

He threw the red-plumed thing far out upon the water. And then he turned to them.

"I have just seen an angel pass—to enter—yonder." A sob closed his throat as he pointed to the sky.

"Her pure blood is on my hands—and, by the help of God, they will shed no more.

"These old guns are playthings—we are broken old men.

"Let us pray."

And there, out in the glare of the awful fiery spectacle, grown weird in the faint white light of a rising sun, arose the voice of prayer—prayer first for forgiveness of false pride and folly—for the women and children—- for the end of the war—for lasting peace.

It was a scene to be remembered. Had anything been lacking in its awful solemnity, it was supplied with a tender potency reaching all hearts, in the knowledge of the dead child, who lay in the little cottage near.

From up and down the levee, as far as the voice had reached, came fervent responses, "Amen!" and "Amen!"

Late in the morning the Riffraffs' artillery, all but their largest gun, was, by the captain's command, dumped into the river.

This reserved cannon they planted, mouth upwards, by the roadside on the site of the tragedy—a fitting memorial of the child-martyr.

It was Mrs. Magwire, who, remembering how Idyl had often stolen out and hung a lantern at this dark turn of the "road bend," began thrusting a pine torch into the cannon's mouth on dark nights as a slight memorial of her. And those who noticed said she took her rosary there and said her beads.

But Captain Doc had soon made the light his own special care, and until his death, ten years later, the old man never failed to supply this beacon to belated travellers on moonless nights.

After a time a large square lantern took the place of the torch of pine, and grateful wayfarers alongshore, by rein or oar, guided or steered by the glimmer of Saint Idyl's Light.

Last year the caving bank carried the rusty gun into the water. It is well that time and its sweet symbol, the peace-loving river, should bury forever from sight all record of a family feud half forgotten.

And yet, is it not meet that when the glorious tale of Farragut's victory is told, the simple story of little Saint Idyl should sometimes follow, as the tender benediction follows the triumphant chant?

"BLINK"

"BLINK"

I

It was nearly midnight of Christmas Eve on Oakland Plantation. In the library of the great house a dim lamp burned, and here, in a big arm-chair before a waning fire, Evelyn Bruce, a fair young girl, sat earnestly talking to a withered old black woman, who sat on the rug at her feet.

"An' yer say de plantatiom done sol', baby, an' we boun' ter move?"

"Yes, mammy, the old place must go."

"An' is de 'Onerble Mr. Citified buyed it, baby? I know he an' ole marster sot up all endurin' las' night a-talkin' and a-figgurin'."

"Yes. Mr. Jacobs has closed the mortgage, and owns the place now."

"An' when is we gwine, baby?"

"The sooner the better. I wish the going were over."

"An' whar'bouts is we gwine, honey?"

"We will go to the city, mammy—to New Orleans. Something tells me that father will never be able to attend to business again, and I am going to work—to make money."

Mammy fell backward. "W-w-w-work! Y-y-you w-w-work! Wh-wh-why, baby, what sort o' funny, cuyus way is you a-talkin', anyhow?"

"Many refined women are earning their living in the city, mammy."

"Is you a-talkin' sense, baby, ur is yer des a-bluffin'? Is yer axed yo' pa yit?"

"I don't think father is well, mammy. He says that whatever I suggest we will do, and I am *sure* it is best. We will take a cheap little house, father and I—"

"Y-y-you an' yo' pa! An' wh-wh-what 'bout me, baby?" Mammy would stammer when she was excited.

"And you, mammy, of course."

"Umh! umh! umh! An' so we gwine ter trabble! An' de' Onerble Mr. Citified done closed de morgans on us! Ef-ef I'd 'a' knowed it dis mornin' when he was a-quizzifyin' me so sergacious, I b'lieve I'd o' upped an' sassed 'im, I des couldn't 'a' helt in. I 'lowed he was teckin' a mighty frien'ly intruss, axin' me do we-all's *puck*on-trees bear big *puck*ons, an'—an' ef de well keep cool all summer, an'—an' he ax me—he ax me—"

"What else did he ask you, mammy?"

"Scuze me namin' it ter yer, baby, but he ax me who was buried in we's graves—he did fur a fac'. Yer reckon dee gwine claim de graves in de morgans, baby?"

Mammy had crouched again at Evelyn's feet, and her eager brown face was now almost against her knee.

"All the land is mortgaged, mammy."

"Don't yer reck'n he mought des nachelly scuze de graves out'n de morgans, baby, ef yer ax 'im mannerly?"

"I'm afraid not, mammy, but after a while we may have them moved."

The old bronze clock on the mantel struck twelve.

"Des listen. De ole clock a-strikin' Chris'mas-gif now. Come 'long, go ter bed, honey. You needs a res', but I ain' gwine sleep none, 'caze all dis heah news what you been a-tellin' me, hit's gwine ter run roun' in my head all night, same as a buzz-saw."

And so they passed out, mammy to her pallet in Evelyn's room, while the sleepless girl stepped to her father's chamber.

Entering on tiptoe, she stood and looked upon his face. He slept as peacefully as a babe. The anxious look of care which he had worn for years had passed away, and the flickering fire revealed the ghost of a smile upon his placid face. In this it was that Evelyn read the truth. The crisis of effort for him was past. He might follow, but he would lead no more.

Since the beginning of the war Colonel Brace's history had been the oft-told tale of loss and disaster, and at the opening of each year since there had been a flaring up of hope and expenditure, then a long summer of wavering promise, followed by an inevitable winter of disappointment.

The old colonel was, both by inheritance and the habit of many successful years, a man of great affairs, and when the crash came he was too old to change. When he bought, he bought heavily. He planted for large results. There was nothing petty about him, not even his debts. And now the end had come.

As Evelyn stood gazing upon his handsome, placid face her eyes were blinded with tears. Falling upon her knees at his side, she engaged for a moment in silent prayer, consecrating herself in love to the life which lay before her, and as she rose she kissed his forehead gently, and passed to her own room.

On the table at her bedside lay several piles of manuscript, and as these attracted her, she turned her chair, and fell to work sorting them into packages, which she laid carefully away.

Evelyn had always loved to scribble, but only within the last few years had she thought of writing for money that she should need. She had already sent several manuscripts to editors of magazines; but somehow, like birds too young to leave the nest, they all found their way back to her. With each failure, however, she had become more determined to succeed, but in the meantime—*now*—she must earn a living. This was not practicable here. In the city all things were possible, and to the city she would go. She would at first accept one of the tempting situations offered in the daily papers, improving her leisure by attending lectures, studying, observing, cultivating herself in every possible way, and after a time she would try her hand again at writing.

It was nearly day when she finally went to bed, but she was up early next morning. There was much to be considered. Many things were to be done.

At first she consulted her father about everything, but his invariable answer, "Just as you say, daughter," transferred all responsibility to her.

A letter to her mother's old New Orleans friend, Madame Le Duc, briefly set forth the circumstances, and asked Madame's aid in securing a small house. Other letters sent in other directions arranged various matters, and Evelyn soon found herself in the vortex of a move. She had a wise, clear head and a steady, resolute hand, and in old mammy a most capable servant. The old woman seemed, indeed, to forget nothing, as she bustled about, packing, suggesting, and, spite of herself, frequently protesting; for, if the truth must be spoken, this move to the city was violating all the traditions of mammy's life.

"Wh-wh-wh-why, baby! Not teck de grime-stone!" she exclaimed one day, in reply to Evelyn's protest against her packing that ponderous article. "How is we gwine sharpen de spade an' de grubbin'-hoe ter work in the gyard'n?"

"We sha'n't have a garden, mammy."

"No gyard'n!" Mammy sat down upon the grindstone in disgust. "Wh-wh-wh-what sort o' a fureign no-groun' place is we gwine ter, anyhow, baby? Honey," she continued, in a troubled voice, "co'se you know I ain't got educatiom, an' I ain't claim knowledge; b-b-b-but ain't you better study on it good 'fo' we goes ter dis heah new country? Dee tells me de cidy's a owdacious place. I been heern a heap o' tales, but I 'ain't say nothin' Is yer done prayed over it good, baby?"

"Yes, dear. I have prayed that we should do only right. What have you heard, mammy?"

"D-d-d-de way folks talks, look like death an' terror is des a-layin' roun' loose in de cidy. Dee tell *me* dat ef yer des nachelly blows out yer light ter go ter bed, dat dis heah some'h'n' what stan' fur wick, hit'll des keep a-sizzin' an' a-sizzin' out, des like sperityal steam; *an' hit's clair pizen!*"

"That is true, mammy. But, you see, we won't blow it out. We'll know better."

"Does yer snuff it out wid snuffers, baby, ur des fling it on de flo' an' tromp yer foots on it?"

"Neither, mammy. The gas comes in through pipes built into the houses, and is turned on and off with a valve, somewhat as we let water out of the refrigerator."

"Um-hm! Well done! Of co'se! On'y, in place o' water what *put out* de light, hit's in'ardly filled wid some'h'n' what *favor* a blaze."

"Exactly."

Mammy reflected a moment. "But de grime-stone gotter stay berhime, is she? An' is we gwine leave all de gyard'n tools an' implemers ter de 'Onerble Mr. Citified?"

"No, mammy; none of the appurtenances of the homestead are mortgaged. We must sell them. We need money, you know."

"What is de impertinences o' de homestid, baby? You forgits I ain't on'erstan' book words."

"Those things intended for family use, mammy. There are the carriage-horses, the cows, the chickens—"

"Bless goodness fur dat! An' who gwine drive 'em inter de cidy fur us, honey?"

"Oh, mammy, we must sell them all."

Mammy was almost crying. "An' what sort o' entry is we gwine meck inter de cidy, honey—empty-handed, same as po' white trash? D-d-don't yer reck'n we b-b-better teck de chickens, baby? Yo' ma thunk a heap o' dem Brahma hens an' dem Clymoth Rockers—dee looks so courageous."

It was hard for Evelyn to refuse. Mammy loved everything on the old place.

"Let us give up all these things now, mammy; and after a while, when I grow rich and famous, I'll buy you all the chickens you want."

At last preparations were over. They were to start on the morrow. Mammy had just returned from a last tour through out-buildings and gardens, and was evidently disturbed.

"Honey," she began, throwing herself on the step at Evelyn's feet, "what yer reck'n? Ole Muffly is a-sett'n' on fo'teen eggs, down in de cotton-seed. W-w-we can't g'way f'm heah an' leave Muffly a-sett'n', hit des nachelly can't be did. D-d-don't yer reck'n dee'd hol' back de morgans a little, till Muffly git done sett'n'?"

It was the same old story. Mammy would never be ready to go.

"But our tickets are bought, mammy."

"An' like as not de 'Onerble Mr. Citified 'll shoo ole Muffly orf de nes' an' spile de whole sett'n'. Tut! tut! tut!" And, groaning in spirit, mammy walked off.

Evelyn had feared, for her father, the actual moment of leaving, and was much relieved when, with his now habitual tranquillity, he smilingly assisted both her and mammy into the sleeper. Instead of entering himself, however, he hesitated.

"Isn't your mother coming, daughter?" he asked, looking backward. "Or—oh, I forgot," he added, quickly. "She has gone on before, hasn't she?"

"Yes, dear, she has gone before," Evelyn answered, hardly knowing what she said, the chill of a new terror upon her.

What did this mean? Was it possible that she had read but half the truth? Was her father's mind not only enfeebled, but going?

Mammy had not heard the question, and so Evelyn bore her anxiety alone, and during the day her anxious eyes were often upon her father's face, but he only smiled and kept silent.

They had been travelling all day, when suddenly, above the rumbling of the train, a weak, bird-like chirp was heard, faint but distinct; and presently it came again, a prolonged "p-e-e-p!"

Heads went up, inquiring faces peered up and down the coach, and fell again to paper or book, when the cry came a third time, and again.

Mammy's face was a study. "'Sh—'sh—'sh! don' say nothin', baby," she whispered, in Evelyn's ear; "but dis heah chicken in my bosom is a-ticklin' me so I can't hardly set still."

Evelyn was absolutely speechless with surprise, as mammy continued by snatches her whispered explanation:

"Des 'fo' we lef' I went 'n' lif' up ole Muffly ter see how de eggs was comin' orn, an' dis heah egg was pipped out, an' de little risindenter look like he eyed me so berseechin' I des nachelly couldn't leave 'im. Look like he knowed he warn't righteously in de morgans, an' 'e crave ter clair out an' trabble. I did hope speech wouldn't come ter 'im tell we got off'n deze heah train kyars."

A halt at a station brought a momentary silence, and right here arose again, clear and shrill, the chicken's cry.

Mammy was equal to the emergency. After glancing inquiringly up and down the coach, she exclaimed, aloud, "Some'h'n' in dis heah kyar soun' des like a vintrilloquer."

"That's just what it is," said an old gentleman opposite, peering around over his spectacles. "And whoever you are, sir, you've been amusing yourself for an hour."

Mammy's ruse had succeeded, and during the rest of the journey, although the chicken developed duly as to vocal powers, the only question asked by the curious was, "Who can the ventriloquist be?"

Evelyn could hardly maintain her self-control, the situation was so utterly absurd.

"I does hope it's a pullet," mammy confided later; "but I doubts it. Hit done struck out wid a mannish movemint a'ready. Muffly's eggs allus hatches out sech invig'rous chickens. I gwine in the dressin'-room, baby, an' wrop 'im up ag'in. Feel like he done kicked 'isse'f loose."

Though she made several trips to the dressing-room in the interest of her hatchling, mammy's serene face held no betrayal of the disturbing secret of her bosom.

At last the journey was over. The train crept with a tired motion into the noisy depot. Then came a rattling ride over cobble-stones, granite, and unpaved streets; a sudden halt before a low-browed cottage; a smiling old lady stepping out to meet them; a slam of the front door—they were at home in New Orleans.

Madame Le Duc seemed to have forgotten nothing that their comfort required, and in many ways that the creole gentlewoman understands so well she was affectionately and unobtrusively kind. And yet, in the life Evelyn was seeking to enter, Madame could give her no aid. About all these new ideas of women—ladies—going out as bread-winners, Madame knew nothing. For twenty years she had gone only to the cathedral, the French Market, the cemetery, and the Chapel of St. Roche. As to all this unconventional American city above Canal Street, it was there and spreading (like the measles and other evils); everybody said so; even her paper, *L'Abeille*, referred to it in French—resentfully. She believed in it historically; but for herself, she "*never travelled,*" *excepting*, as she quaintly put it, in her "*acquaintances*"—the French streets with which she was familiar.

The house she had selected was a typical old-fashioned French cottage, venerable in scaling plaster and fern-tufted tile roof, but cool and roomy within as uninviting without. A small inland garden surprised the eye as one entered the battened gate at its side, and a dormer-window in the roof looked out upon the rigging of ships at anchor but a stone's-throw away.

Here, to the chamber above, Evelyn led her father. Furnishing this large upper room with familiar objects, and pointing out the novelties of the view from its window, she tried to interpret his new life happily for him, and he smiled, and seemed content.

It was surprising to see how soon mammy fell into line with the changed order of things. The French Market, with its "cuyus fureign folks an' mixed talk," was a panorama of daily unfolding wonders to her. "But huccome dee calls it French?" she exclaimed, one day. "I been listenin' good, an' I hear 'em jabber, jabber, jabber all dey fanciful lingoes, but I 'ain't heern nair one say *polly fronsay*, an' yit I know dats de riverend book French." The Indian squaws in the market, sitting flat on the ground, surrounded by their wares, she held in special contempt. "I holds myse'f *clair* 'bove a Injun," she boasted. "Dee ain't look jinnywine ter me. Dee ain't nuther white folks nur niggers, nair one. Sett'n' deeselves up fur go-betweens, an' sellin' sech grass-greens as we lef' berhindt us growin' in de wilderness!"

But one unfailing source of pleasure to mammy was the little chicken, "Blink," who, she declared, "named 'isse'f Blink de day he blinked at me so cunnin' out'n de shell. Blink 'ain't said nothin' wid 'is mouf," she continued, eying him proudly, "'caze he know eye-speech set on a chicken a heap better'n human words, mo' inspecial on a yo'ng half-hatched chicken like Blink was dat day, cramped wid de egg-shell behime an' de morgans starin' 'im in de face befo', an' not knowin' how he gwine come out'n his trouble. He des kep' silence, an' wink all 'is argimints, an' 'e wink to the p'int, too!"

In spite of his unique entrance into the world and his precarious journey, Blink was a vigorous young chicken, with what mammy was pleased to call "a good proud step an' knowin' eyes."

Three months passed. The long, dull summer was approaching, and yet Evelyn had found no regular employment. She had not been idle. Sewing for the market folk, decorating palmetto fans and Easter eggs, which mammy peddled in the big houses, she had earned small sums of money from time to time. In her enforced leisure she found opportunity for study, and her picturesque surroundings were as an open book.

Impressions of the quaint old French and Spanish city, with its motley population, were carefully jotted down in her note-book. These first descriptions she afterwards rewrote, discarding weakening detail, elaborating the occasional triviality which seemed to reflect the true local tint—a nice distinction, involving conscientious hard work. How she longed for criticism and advice!

A year ago her father, now usually dozing in his chair while she worked, would have been a most able and affectionate critic; but now—She rejoiced when a day passed without his asking for her mother, and wondering why she did not come.

And so it was that in her need of sympathy Evelyn began to read her writings, some of which had grown into stories, to mammy. The very exercise of reading aloud—the sound of it—was helpful. That mammy's criticisms should have proven valuable in themselves was a surprise, but it was even so.

II

"A pusson would know dat was fanciful de way hit reads orf, des like a pusson 'magine some'h'n' what ain't so."

Such was mammy's first criticism of a story which had just come back, returned from an editor. Evelyn had been trying to discover wherein its weakness lay.

Mammy had caught the truth. The story was unreal. The English seemed good, the construction fair, but—it was *"fanciful."*

The criticism set Evelyn to thinking. She laid aside this, and read another manuscript aloud.

"I tell yer, honey, a-a-a pusson 'd know you had educatiom, de way you c'n fetch in de dictionary words."

"Don't you understand them, mammy?" she asked, quickly, catching another idea.

"Who, me? Law, baby, I don't crave ter on'erstan' all dat granjer. I des ketches de chune, an' hit sho is got a glorified ring."

Here was a valuable hint. She must simplify her style. The tide of popular writing was, she knew, in the other direction, but the *best* writing was *simple*.

The suggestion sent her back to study.

And now for her own improvement she rewrote the "story of big words" in the simplest English she could command, bidding mammy tell her if there was one word she could not understand.

In the transition the spirit of the story was necessarily changed, but the exercise was good. Mammy understood every word.

"But, baby," she protested, with a troubled face, "look like *hit don't stan' no mo'*; all its granjer done gone. You better fix it up des like it was befo', honey. Hit 'minds me o' some o' deze heah fine folks what walks de streets. You know *folks what 'ain't got nothin' else*, dee des nachelly *'bleege* ter put on finery."

How clever mammy was! How wholesome the unconscious satire of her criticism! This story, shorn of its grandeur, could not stand indeed. It was weak and affected.

"You dear old mammy," exclaimed Evelyn, "you don't know how you are helping me."

"Gord knows I wushes I could holp you, honey. I 'ain't nuver is craved educatiom befo', but now, look like I'd like ter be king of all de smartness, an' know all dey is in de books. I wouldn't hol' back *noth'n* f'om yer, baby."

And Evelyn knew it was true.

"Look ter me, baby," mammy suggested, another night, after listening to a highly imaginative story—"look ter me like ef—ef—ef you'd des write down some *truly truth* what is *ac-chilly happened*, an' glorify it wid educatiom, hit 'd des nachelly stan' in a book."

"I've been thinking of that," said Evelyn, reflectively, laying aside her manuscript.

"How does this sound, mammy?" she asked, a week later, when, taking up an unfinished tale, she began to read.

It was the story of their own lives, dating from the sale of the plantation. The names, of course, were changed, excepting Blink's, and, indeed, until he appeared upon the scene, although mammy listened breathless, she did not recognize the characters. Blink, however, was unmistakable, and when he announced himself from the old woman's bosom his identity flashed upon mammy, and she tumbled over on the floor, laughing and crying alternately. Evelyn had written from her heart, and the story, simply told, held all the wrench of parting with old associations, while the spirit of courage and hope, which animated her, breathed in every line as she described their entrance upon their new life.

"My heart was teched f'om de fus't, baby," said mammy, presently, wiping her eyes; "b-b-b-but look heah, honey, I'd—I'd be wuss'n a hycoprite ef I let dat noble ole black 'oman, de way you done specified 'er, stan' fur me. Y-y-yer got ter change all dat, honey. Dey warn't nothin' on top o' dis roun' worl' what fetched me 'long wid y' all but 'cep' 'caze I des *nachelly love yer*, an' all dat book granjer what you done laid on me I *don' know nothin' 't all about it*, an' yer got ter *teck it orf*, an' write me down like I is, des a po' ole nigger wha' done fell in wid de Gord-blessedes' white folks wha' ever lived on dis earth, an'—an' wha' gwine *foller* 'em an' *stay by 'em*, don' keer which-a-way dee go, so long as 'er ole han's is able ter holp 'em. Yer got ter change all dat, honey.

"But Blink! De laws-o'-mussy! Maybe hit's 'caze I been hatched 'im an' raised 'im, but look ter me like he ain't no *dis*grace ter de story, no way. Seem like he sets orf de book. Yer ain't gwine say nothin' 'bout Blink bein' a frizzly, is yer? 'Twouldn't do no good ter tell it on 'im."

"I didn't know it, mammy."

"Yas, indeedy. Po' Blink's feathers done taken on a secon' twis'." She spoke, with maternal solicitude. "I d'know huccome he come dat-a-way, 'caze we 'ain't nuver is had no frizzly stock 'mongs' our chickens. Sometimes I b'lieve Blink tumbled 'isse'f up dat-a-way tryin' ter wriggle 'isse'f outn de morgans. I hates it mightily. Look like a frizzly can't put on grandeur no way, don' keer how mannerly 'e hol' 'isse'f."

The progress of the new story, which mammy considered under her especial supervision, was now her engrossing thought.

"Yer better walk straight, Blink," she would exclaim—"yer better walk straight an' step high, 'caze yer gwine in a book, honey, 'long wid de aristokercy!"

One day Blink walked leisurely in from the street, returning, happily for mammy's peace of mind, before he had been missed. He raised his wings a moment as he entered, as if pleased to get home, and mammy exclaimed, as she burst out laughing:

"Don't you come in heah shruggin' yo' shoulders at me, Blink, an' puttin' on no French airs. I believe Blink been out teckin' French lessons." She took her pet into her arms. "Is you crave ter learn fureign speech, Blinky, like de res' o' dis mixed-talkin' settle*mint*? Is you 'shamed o' yo' country voice, honey, an' tryin' ter ketch a French crow? No, he ain't," she added, putting him down at last, but watching him fondly. "Blink know he's a Bruce. An' he know he's folks is in tribulatiom, an' hilarity ain't become 'im—dat's huccome Blink 'ain't crowed none—*ain't it, Blink*?"

And Blink wisely winked his knowing eyes. That he had, indeed, never proclaimed his roosterhood by crowing was a source of some anxiety to mammy.

"Maybe Blink don't know he's a rooster," she confided to Evelyn one day. "Sho 'nough, honey, he nuver is seen none! De neares' ter 'isse'f what he knows is dat ole green polly what set in de fig-tree nex' do', an' talk Gascon. I seed Blink 'is*tid*day stan' an' look at' im, an' den look down at 'isse'f, same as ter say, 'Is I a polly, or what?' An' den 'e open an' shet 'is mouf, like 'e tryin' ter twis' it, polly fashion, an' hit won't twis', an' den 'e des shaken 'is head, an' walk orf, like 'e heavy-hearted an' mixed in 'is mind. Blink don't know what 'spornsibility lay on 'im ter keep our courage up. You heah me, Blink! Open yo' mouf, an' crow out, like a man!"

But Blink was biding his time.

During this time, in spite of strictest economy, money was going out faster than it came in.

"I tell yer what I been thinkin', baby," said mammy, as she and Evelyn discussed the situation. "I think de bes' thing you can do is ter hire me out. I can cook you alls breckfus' soon, an' go out an' make day's work, an' come home plenty o' time ter cook de little speck o' dinner you an' ole boss needs."

"Oh no, no! You mustn't think of it, mammy."

"But what we gwine do, baby? We des *can't* get out'n *money*. Hit *won't do*!"

"Maybe I should have taken that position as lady's companion, mammy."

"An' stay 'way all nights f'om yo' pa, when you de onlies' light ter 'is eyes? No, no, honey!"

"But it has been my only offer, and sometimes I think—"

"Hush talkin' dat-a-way, baby. Don't yer pray? An' don't yer trus' Gord? An' ain't yer done walked de streets tell you mos' drapped down, lookin' fur work? An' can't yer teck de hint dat de Lord done laid off yo' work *right heah in the house*? You go 'long now, an' cheer up yo' pa, des like you been doin', an' study yo' books, an' write down true joy an' true sorrer in yo' stories, an' glorify Gord wid yo' sense, an' don't pester yo'se'f 'bout to-day an' to-morrer, an'—an'—an' ef de gorspil is de trufe, an'—an' ef a po' ole nigger's prayers mounts ter heaven on de wings o' faith, Gord ain't gwine let a hair o' yo' head perish."

But mammy pondered in her heart much concerning the financial outlook, and it was on the day after this conversation that she dressed herself with unusual care, and, without announcing her errand, started out.

Her return soon brought its own explanation, however, for upon her old head she bore a huge bundle of unlaundered clothing.

"What in the world!" exclaimed Evelyn; but before she could voice a protest, mammy interrupted her.

"Nuver you mind, baby! I des waked up," she exclaimed, throwing her bundle at the kitchen door. "I been preachin' ter you 'bout teckin' hints, an' 'ain't been readin' my own lesson. Huccome we got dis heah nice sunny back yard, an' dis bustin' cisternful o' rain-water? Huccome de boa'din'-house folks at de corner keeps a-passin' an' a-passin' by dis gate wid all dey fluted finery on, ef 'twarn't ter gimme a hint dat dey's wealth a-layin' at de do', an' me, bline as a bat, 'ain't seen it?"

"Oh, but, mammy, you can't take in washing. You are too old; it is too hard. You *mustn't*—"

"Ef-ef-ef-ef you gits obstropulous, I-I-I gwine whup yer, sho. Y-y-yer know how much money's a-comin' out'n dat bundle, baby? *Five dollars!*" This in a stage-whisper. "An' not a speck o' dirt on nothin'; des baby caps an' lace doin's rumpled up."

"How did you manage it, mammy?"

"Well, baby, I des put on my fluted ap'on—an' you know it's ironed purty—an' my clair-starched neck-hankcher, an'—an' *my business face*, an' I helt up my head an' walked in, an' axed good prices, an' de ladies, dee des tooken took one good look at me, an' gimme all I'd carry. You know washin' an' ironin' is my pleasure, baby."

It was useless to protest, and so, after a moment, Evelyn began rolling up her sleeves.

"I am going to help you, mammy," she said, quietly but firmly; but before she could protest, mammy had gathered her into her arms, and carried her into her own room. Setting her down at her desk, she exclaimed:

"Now, ef *you* goes ter de wash-tub, dey ain't nothin' lef fur *me* ter do but 'cep'n' ter *set down an' write de story*, an' you know I can't do it."

"But, mammy, I *must* help you."

"Is you gwine *meck* me whup yer, whe'r ur no, baby? Now I gwine meck a bargain wid yer. *You* set down an' write, an' *I* gwine play de pianner on de washboa'd, an' to-night you can read off what yer done put down, an' ef yer done written it purty an' sweet, you can come an' turn de flutin'-machine fur me ter-morrer. Yer gwine meck de bargain wid me, baby?"

Evelyn was so touched that she had not voice to answer. Rising from her seat, she put her arms around mammy's neck and kissed her old face, and as she turned away a tear rolled down her cheek. And so the "bargain" was sealed.

Before going to her desk Evelyn went to her father, to see that he wanted nothing. He sat, as usual, gazing silently out of the window.

"Daughter," said he, as she entered, "are we in France?"

"No, dear," she answered, startled at the question.

"But the language I hear in the street is French; and see the ship-masts—French flags flying. But there is the German too, and English, and last week there was a Scandinavian. Where are we truly, daughter? My surroundings confuse me."

"We are in New Orleans, father—in the French Quarter. Ships from almost everywhere come to this port, you know. Let us walk out to the levee this morning, and see the men-of-war in the river. The air will revive you."

"Well, if your mother comes. She might come while we were away."

And so it was always. With her heart trembling within her, Evelyn went to her desk. "Surely," she thought, "there is much need that I shall do my best." Almost reverentially she took her pen, as she proceeded with the true story she had begun.

"I done changed my min' 'bout dat ole 'oman wha' stan' fur me, baby," said mammy that night. "You leave 'er des like she is. She glorifies de story a heap better'n my nachel self could do it. I been a-thinkin' 'bout it, an' *de finer that ole 'oman ac'*, an' de mo' granjer yer lay on 'er, de better yer gwine meck de book, 'caze de ole gemplum wha' stan' fur ole marster, his times an' seasons is done past, an' he can't do nothin' but set still an' wait, an'—an' de yo'ng missus, she ain't fitten ter wrastle on de outskirts; she ain't nothin' but 'cep' des a lovin' sweet saint, wid 'er face set ter a high, far mark—"

"Hush, mammy!"

"*I'm a-talkin' 'bout de book, baby, an' don't you interrup' me no mo'!* An' *I say ef dis ole 'oman wha' stan' fur me, ef-ef-ef she got a weak spot in 'er, dey won't be no story to it.* She de one wha' got ter *stan' by de battlemints an' hol' de fort.*"

"That's just what you are doing, mammy. There isn't a grain in her that is finer than you."

"'Sh! dis ain't no time fur foolishness, baby. Yer 'ain't said nothin' 'bout yo' ma an' de ole black 'oman's baby bein' borned de same day, is yer? An' how de ole 'oman nussed 'em bofe des like twins? An'—an' how folks 'cused 'er o' starvin' 'er own baby on de 'count o' yo' ma bein' puny? (*But dat warn't true.*) Maybe yer better leave all dat out, 'caze hit mought spile de story."

"How could it spoil it, mammy?"

"Don't yer see, ef folks knowed dat dem white folks an' dat ole black 'oman was *dat close-t,* dey wouldn't be no principle in it. Dey ain't nothin' but *love* in *dat,* an' de ole 'oman *couldn't he'p 'erse'f, no mo'n I could he'p it!* No right-minded pusson is gwine ter deny dey own heart. Yer better leave all dat out, honey. B-b-but deys some'h'n' else wha' been lef out, wha' b'long in de book. Yer 'ain't named de way de little mistus sot up all nights an' nussed de ole 'oman time she was sick, an'—an'—an' de way she sew all de ole 'oman's cloze; an'—an'—an' yer done lef' out a heap o' de purtiness an' de sweetness o' de yo'ng mistus! Dis is a book, baby, an'—an'—yer boun' ter do jestice!"

In this fashion the story was written.

"And what do you think I am going to do with it, mammy?" said Evelyn, when finally, having done her very best, she was willing to call it finished.

"Yer know some'h'n' baby? Ef-ef-ef I had de money, look like I'd buy that story myse'f. Seem some way like I loves it. Co'se I couldn't read it; but my min' been on it so long, seem like, ef I'd study de pages good dee'd open up ter me. What yer gwine do wid it, baby?"

"Oh, mammy, I can hardly tell you! My heart seems in my throat when I dare to think of it; but *I'm going to try it*. A New York magazine has offered five hundred dollars for a best story—*five hundred dollars*! Think, mammy, what it would do for us!"

"Dat wouldn't buy de plantatiom back, would it, baby?" Mammy had no conception of large sums.

"We don't want it back, mammy. It would pay for moving our dear ones to graves of their own; we should put a nice sum in bank; you shouldn't do any more washing; and if we can write one good story, you know we can write more. It will be only a beginning."

"An' I tell yer what I gwine do. I gwine pray over it good, des like I been doin' f'om de start, an' ef hit's Gord's will, dem folks 'll be moved in de sperit ter sen' 'long de money."

And so the story was sent.

After it was gone the atmosphere seemed brighter. The pending decision was now a fixed point to which all their hopes were directed.

The very audacity of the effort seemed inspiration to more ambitious work; and during the long summer, while in her busy hands the fluting-machine went round and round, Evelyn's mind was full of plans for the future.

Finally, December, with its promise of the momentous decision, was come, and Evelyn found herself full of anxious misgivings.

What merit entitling it to special consideration had the little story? Did it bear the impress of self-forgetful, conscientious purpose, or was this a thing only feebly struggling into life within herself—not yet the compelling force that indelibly stamps itself upon the earnest labor of consecrated hands? How often in the silent hours of night did she ask herself questions like these!

At last it was Christmas Eve again, and Saturday night. When the days are dark, what is so depressing as an anniversary—an anniversary joyous in its very essence? How one Christmas brings in its train memory-pictures of those gone before!

This had been a hard day for Evelyn. Her heart felt weak within her, and yet, realizing that she alone represented youth and hope in the little household, and feeling need that her own courage should be sustained, she had been more than usually merry all day. She had clandestinely prepared little surprises for her father and mammy, and was both amused and touched to discover the old woman secreting mysterious little parcels which she knew were to come to her in the morning.

"Wouldn't it be funny if, after all, I should turn out to be only a good washerwoman, mammy?" she said, laughing, as she assisted the old woman in pinning up a basket of laundered clothing.

"Hit'd be funnier yit ef *I'd* turn out inter one o' deze heah book-writers, wouldn't it?" And mammy laughed heartily at her own joke. "Look like I better study my a-b abs fus', let 'lone puttin' 'em back on paper wid a pen. I tell you educatiom's a-spreadin' in dis fam'ly, sho. Time Blink run over de sheet out a-bleachin' 'is*tid*dy, he written a Chinese letter all over it. Didn't you, Blink? What de matter wid Blink anyhow, to-day?" she added, taking the last pin from her head-kerchief. "Blink look like he nervous some way dis evenin'. He keep a-walkin' roun', an' winkin' so slow, an' retchin' his neck out de back-do' so cuyus. Stop a-battin' yo' eyes at me, Blink! Ef yo' got some'h'n' ter say, *say it*!"

A sudden noisy rattle of the iron door-knocker—mammy trotting to the door—the postman—a letter! It all happened in a minute.

How Evelyn's heart throbbed and her hand trembled as she opened the envelope! "Oh, mammy!" she cried, trembling now like an aspen leaf. "*Thank God!*"

"Is dee d-d-d-done sont de money, baby?" Her old face was twitching too.

But Evelyn could not answer. Nodding her head, she fell sobbing on mammy's shoulder.

Mammy raised her apron to her eyes, and there's no telling what "foolishness" she might have committed had it not been that suddenly, right at her side, arose a most jubilant screech.

Blink, perched on the handle of the clothes-basket, was crowing with all his might.

Evelyn, startled, raised her head, and laughed through her tears, while mammy threw herself at full length upon the floor, shouting aloud.

"Tell me chickens 'ain't got secon'-sight! Blink see'd—he see'd—Laws-o'-mussy, baby, look yonder at dat little yaller rooster stan'in' on de fence. *Dat what Blink see. Co'se it is!*"

DUKE'S CHRISTMAS

DUKE'S CHRISTMAS

"You des gimme de white folks's Christmas-dinner plates, time they git thoo eatin', an' lemme scrape 'em in a pan, an' set dat pan in my lap, an' blow out de light, an' *go it bline*! Hush, honey, hush, while I shet my eyes now an' tas'e all de samples what'd come out'n dat pan—cramberries, an' tukkey-stuffin' wid *puck*ons in it, an' ham an' fried oyscher an'—an' minch-meat, an' chow-chow pickle an'—an' jelly! Umh! Don' keer which-a-one I strack fust—dey all got de Christmas seasonin'!"

Old Uncle Mose closed his eyes and smiled, even smacked his lips in contemplation of the imaginary feast which he summoned at will from his early memories. Little Duke, his grandchild, sitting beside him on the floor, rolled his big eyes and looked troubled. Black as a raven, nine years old and small of his age, but agile and shrewd as a little fox, he was at present the practical head of this family of two.

This state of affairs had existed for more than two months, ever since a last attack of rheumatism had lifted his grandfather's leg upon the chair before him and held it there.

Duke's success as a provider was somewhat remarkable, considering his size, color, and limited education.

True, he had no rent to pay, for their one-roomed cabin, standing on uncertain stilts outside the old levee, had been deserted during the last high-water, when Uncle Mose had "tooken de chances" and moved in. But then Mose had been able to earn his seventy-five cents a day at wood-sawing; and besides, by keeping his fishing-lines baited and set out the back and front doors—there were no windows—he had often drawn in a catfish, or his shrimp-bag had yielded breakfast for two.

Duke's responsibilities had come with the winter and its greater needs, when the receding waters had withdrawn even the small chance of landing a dinner with hook and line. True, it had been done on several occasions, when Duke had come home to find fricasseed chickens for dinner; but somehow the neighbors' chickens had grown wary, and refused to be enticed by the corn that lay under Mose's cabin.

The few occasions when one of their number, swallowing an innocent-looking grain, had been suddenly lifted up into space, disappearing through the floor above, seemed to have impressed the survivors.

Mose was a church-member, and would have scorned to rob a hen-roost, but he declared "when strange chickens come a-foolin' roun' bitin' on my fish-lines, I des twisses dey necks ter put 'em out'n dey misery."

It had been a long time since he had met with any success at this poultry-fishing, and yet he always kept a few lines out.

He *professed* to be fishing for crawfish—as if crawfish ever bit on a hook or ate corn! Still, it eased his conscience, for he did try to set his grandson a Christian example consistent with his precepts.

It was Christmas Eve, and the boy felt a sort of moral responsibility in the matter of providing a suitable Christmas dinner for the morrow. His question as to what the old man would like to have had elicited the enthusiastic bit of reminiscence with which this story opens. Here was a poser! His grandfather had described just the identical kind of dinner which he felt powerless to procure. If he had said oysters, or chicken, or even turkey, Duke thought he could have managed it; but a pan of rich fragments was simply out of the question.

"Wouldn't you des as lief have a pone o' hot egg-bread, gran'dad, an'—an'—an' maybe a nice baked chicken—ur—ur a—"

"Ur a nothin', boy! Don't talk to me! I'd a heap'd ruther have a secon'-han' white Christmas dinner 'n de bes' fus'-han' nigger one you ever seed, an' I ain't no spring-chicken, nuther. I done had 'spe'unce o' Christmas dinners. An' what you talkin' 'bout, anyhow? Whar you gwine git roas' chicken, nigger?"

"I don' know, less'n I'd meck a heap o' money to-day; but I could sho' git a whole chicken ter roas' easier'n I could git dat pan full o' goodies *you's* a-talkin' 'bout.

"Is you gwine crawfishin' to-day, gran'daddy?" he continued, cautiously, rolling his eyes. "'Caze when I cross de road, terreckly, I gwine shoo off some o' dem big fat hens dat scratches up so much dus'. Dey des a puffec' nuisance, scratchin' dus' clean inter my eyes ev'y time I go down de road."

"Dey is, is dey? De nasty, impident things! You better not shoo none of 'em over heah, less'n you want me ter wring dey necks—which I boun' ter do ef dey pester my crawfish-lines."

"Well, I'm gwine now, gran'dad. Ev'ything is done did an' set whar you kin reach—I gwine down de road an' shoo dem sassy chickens away. Dis here bucket o' brick-dus' sho' is heavy," he added, as he lifted to his head a huge pail.

Starting out, he gathered up a few grains of corn, dropping them along in his wake until he reached the open where the chickens were; when, making a circuit round them, he drove them slowly until he saw them begin to pick up the corn. Then he turned, whistling as he went, into a side street, and proceeded on his way.

Old Mose chuckled audibly as Duke passed out, and, baiting his lines with corn and scraps of meat, he lifted the bit of broken plank from the floor, and set about his day's sport.

"Now, Mr. Chicken, I'm settin' deze heah lines fur crawfish, an' ef you smarties come a-foolin' round 'em, I gwine punish you 'cordin' ter de law. You heah me!" He chuckled as he thus presented his defence anew before the bar of his own conscience.

But the chickens did not bite to-day—not a mother's son or daughter of them—though they ventured cautiously to the very edge of the cabin.

It was a discouraging business, and the day seemed very long. It was nearly nightfall when Mose recognized Duke's familiar whistle from the levee. And when he heard the little bare feet pattering on the single plank that led from the brow of the bank to the cabin-door, he coughed and chuckled as if to disguise a certain eager agitation that always seized him when the little boy came home at night.

"Here me," Duke called, still outside the door; adding as he entered, while he set his pail beside the old man, "How you is to-night, gran'dad?"

"Des po'ly, thank Gord. How you yo'se'f, my man?" There was a note of affection in the old man's voice as he addressed the little pickaninny, who seemed in the twilight a mere midget.

"An' what you got dyah?" he continued, turning to the pail, beside which Duke knelt, lighting a candle.

"*Picayune* o' light bread an' *lagniappe* o' salt," Duke began, lifting out the parcels, "an' *picayune* o' molasses an' *lagniappe* o' coal-ile, ter rub yo' leg wid— heah hit in de tin can—an' *picayune* o' coffee an' *lagniappe* o' matches—heah dey is, fo'teen an' a half, but de half ain't got no fizz on it. An' deze heah in de bottom, dey des chips I picked up 'long de road."

"An' you ain't axed fur no *lagniappe* fo' yo'self, Juke. Whyn't you ax fur des one *lagniappe* o' sugar-plums, baby, bein's it's Christmas? Yo' ole gran'dad 'ain't got nothin' fur you, an' you know to-morrer is sho 'nough Christmas, boy. I 'ain't got even ter say a crawfish bite on my lines to-day, much less'n some'h'n' fittin' fur a Christmas-gif'. I did set heah an' whittle you a little whistle, but some'h'n' went wrong wid it. Hit won't blow. But tell me, how's business to-day, boy? I see you done sol' yo' brick-dus'?"

"Yas, sir, but I toted it purty nigh all day 'fo' I *is* sold it. De folks wherever I went dey say nobody don't want to scour on Christmas Eve. An' one time I set it down an' made three nickels cuttin' grass an' holdin' a white man's horse, an' dat gimme a res'. An' I started out ag'in, an' I walked inter a big house an' ax de lady ain't she want ter buy some pounded brick. An', gran'dad, you know what meck she buy it? 'Caze she say my bucket is mos' as big as I is, an' ef I had de grit ter tote it clean ter her house on Christmas Eve, she say I sha'n't pack it back—an' she gimme a dime fur it, too, stid a nickel. An' she gimme two hole-in-de-middle cakes, wid sugar on 'em. Heah dey is." Duke took two sorry-lookin' rings from his hat and presented them to the old man. "I done et de sugar off 'em," he continued. "'Caze I knowed it'd give you de toofache in yo' gums. An' I tol' 'er what you say, gran'dad!"

Mose turned quickly.

"What you tol' dat white lady I say, nigger?"

"I des tol' 'er what you say 'bout scrapin' de plates into a pan."

Mose grinned broadly. "Is you had de face ter tell dat strange white 'oman sech talk as dat? An' what she say?"

"She des looked at me up an' down fur a minute, an' den she broke out in a laugh, an' she say: 'You sho' is de littles' coon I ever seen out foragin'!' An' wid dat she say: 'Ef you'll come roun' to-morrer night, 'bout dark, I'll give you as big a pan o' scraps as you kin tote.'"

There were tears in the old man's eyes, and he actually giggled.

"Is she? Well done! But ain't you 'feerd you'll los' yo'self, gwine 'way down town at night?"

"Los' who, gran'dad? You can't los' me in dis city, so long as de red-light Pertania cars is runnin'. I kin ketch on berhine tell dey fling me off, den teck de nex' one tell dey fling me off ag'in—an' hit ain't so fur dat-a-way."

"Does dey fling yer off rough, boy? Look out dey don't bre'k yo' bones!"

"Dey ain't gwine crack none o' my bones. Sometimes de drivers kicks me off, an' sometimes dey cusses me off, tell I lets go des ter save Gord's name—dat's a fac'."

"Dat's right. Save it when you kin, boy. So she gwine scrape de Christmas plates fur me, is she? I wonder what sort o' white folks dis here tar-baby o' mine done strucken in wid, anyhow? You sho' dey reel quality white folks, is yer, Juke? 'Caze I ain't gwine sile my mouf on no po' white-trash scraps."

"I ain't no sho'er'n des what I tell yer, gran'dad. Ef dey ain't quality, I don' know nothin' 't all 'bout it. I tell yer when I walked roun' dat yard clean ter de kitchen on dem flag-stones wid dat bucket o' brick on my hade, I had ter stop an' ketch my bref fo' I could talk, an' de cook, a sassy, fat, black lady, she would o' sont me out, but de madam, she seed me 'erse'f, an' she tooken took notice ter me, an' tell me set my bucket down, an' de yo'ng ladies, beatin' eggs in de kitchen, dey was makin' sport o' me, too—ax' me is I weaned yit, an' one ob 'em ax me is my nuss los' me! Den dey gimme deze heah hole-in-de-middle cakes, an' some reesons. I des fotched you a few reesons, but I done et de mos' ob em—I ain't gwine tell you no lie about it."

"Dat's right, baby. I'm glad you is et 'em—des so dey don't cramp yer up—an' come 'long now an' eat yo' dinner. I saved you a good pan o' greens an' meat. What else is you et to-day, boy?"

"De ladies in de kitchen dey gimme two burnt cakes, an' I swapped half o' my reesons wid a white boy for a biscuit—but I sho is hongry."

"Yas, an' you sleepy, too—I know you is."

"But I gwine git up soon, gran'dad. One market-lady she seh ef I come early in de mornin' an' tote baskits home, she gwine gimme some'h'n' good; an' I'm gwine ketch all dem butchers and fish-ladies in dat Mag'zine Markit 'Christmas-gif'!' An' I bet yer dey'll gimme some'h'n' ter fetch home. Las' Christmas I got seven nickels an' a whole passel o' marketin' des a-ketchin' 'em Christmas-gif'. Deze heah black molasses I brung yer home to-night—how yer like 'em, gran'dad?"

"Fust-rate, boy. Don't yer see me eatin' 'em? Say yo' pra'rs now, Juke, an' lay down, 'caze I gwine weck you up by sun-up."

It was not long before little Duke was snoring on his pallet, when old Mose, reaching behind the mantel, produced a finely braided leather whip, which he laid beside the sleeping boy.

"Wush't I had a apple ur orwange ur stick o' candy ur some'h'n' sweet ter lay by 'im fur Christmas," he said, fondly, as he looked upon the little sleeping figure. "Reck'n I mought bile dem molasses down inter a little candy—seem lak hit's de onlies' chance dey is."

And turning back to the low fire, Mose stirred the coals a little, poured the remains of Duke's "*picayune* o' molasses" into a tomato-can, and began his labor of love.

Like much of such service, it was for a long time simply a question of waiting; and Mose found it no simple task, even when it had reached the desired point, to pull the hot candy to a fairness of complexion approaching whiteness. When, however, he was able at last to lay a heavy, copper-colored twist with the whip beside the sleeping boy, he counted the trouble as nothing; and hobbling over to his own cot, he was soon also sleeping.

The sun was showing in a gleam on the river next morning when Mose called, lustily, "Weck up, Juke, weck up! Christmas-gif', boy, Christmas-gif'!"

Duke turned heavily once; then, catching the words, he sprang up with a bound.

"Christmas-gif', gran'dad!" he returned, rubbing his eyes; then fully waking, he cried, "Look onder de chips in de bucket, gran'dad."

And the old man choked up again as he produced the bag of tobacco, over which he had actually cried a little last night when he had found it hidden beneath the chips with which he had cooked Duke's candy.

"I 'clare, Juke, I 'clare you is a caution," was all he could say.

"An' who gimme all deze?" Duke exclaimed, suddenly seeing his own gifts.

"I don' know nothin' 't all 'bout it, less'n ole Santa Claus mought o' tooken a rest in our mud chimbley las' night," said the old man, between laughter and tears.

And Duke, the knowing little scamp, cracking his whip, munching his candy and grinning, replied:

"I s'pec' he is, gran'dad; an' I s'pec' he come down an' b'iled up yo' nickel o' molasses, too, ter meck me dis candy. Tell yer, dis whup, she's got a daisy snapper on 'er, gran'dad! She's wuth a dozen o' deze heah white-boy *w'ips*, she is!"

The last thing Mose heard as Duke descended the levee that morning was the crack of the new whip; and he said, as he filled his pipe, "De idee o' dat little tar-baby o' mine fetchin' me a Christmas-gif'!"

It was past noon when Duke got home again, bearing upon his shoulder, like a veritable little Santa Claus himself, a half-filled coffee-sack, the joint results of his service in the market and of the generosity of its autocrats.

The latter had evidently measured their gratuities by the size of their beneficiary, as their gifts were very small. Still, as the little fellow emptied the sack upon the floor, they made quite a tempting display. There were oranges, apples, bananas, several of each; a bunch of soup-greens, scraps of fresh meat—evidently butchers' "trimmings"—odds and ends of vegetables; while in the midst of the melee three live crabs struck out in as many directions for freedom.

They were soon landed in a pot; while Mose, who was really no mean cook, was preparing what seemed a sumptuous mid-day meal.

Late in the afternoon, while Mose nodded in his chair, Duke sat in the open doorway, stuffing the last banana into his little stomach, which was already as tight as a kettle-drum. He had cracked his whip until he was tired, but he still kept cracking it. He cracked it at every fly that lit on the floor, at the motes that floated into the shaft of sunlight before him, at special knots in the door-sill, or at nothing, as the spirit moved him. A sort of holiday feeling, such as he felt on Sundays, had kept him at home this afternoon. If he had known that to be a little too full of good things and a little tired of cracking whips or tooting horns or drumming was the happy condition of most of the rich boys of the land at that identical moment, he could not have been more content than he was. If his stomach ached just a little, he thought of all the good things in it, and was rather pleased to have it ache—just this little. It emphasized his realization of Christmas.

As the evening wore on, and the crabs and bananas and molasses-candy stopped arguing with one another down in his little stomach, he found himself thinking, with some pleasure, of the pan of scraps he was to get for his grandfather, and he wished for the hour when he should go. He was glad when at last the old man waked with a start and began talking to him.

"I been wushin' you'd weck up an' talk, gran'dad," he said, "caze I wants ter ax yer what's all dis here dey say 'bout Christmas? When I was comin' 'long to-day I stopped in a big chu'ch, an' dey was a preacher-man standin' up wid a white night-gown on, an' he say dis here's our Lord's birfday. I heerd 'im say it myse'f. Is dat so?"

"Co'se it is, Juke. Huccome you ax me sech ignunt questions? Gimme dat Bible, boy, an' lemme read you some 'ligion."

Mose had been a sort of lay-preacher in his day, and really could read a little, spelling or stumbling over the long words. Taking the book reverently, he leaned forward until the shaft of sunlight fell upon the open page, when with halting speech he read to the little boy, who listened with open-mouthed attention, the story of the birth at Bethlehem.

"An' look heah, Juke, my boy," he said, finally, closing the book, "hit's been on my min' all day ter tell yer I ain't gwine fishin' no mo' tell de high-water come back—you heah? 'Caze yer know somebody's chickens *mought* come an' pick up de bait, an' I'd be bleeged ter kill 'em ter save 'em, an' we ain' gwine do dat no mo', me an' you. You heah, Juke?"

Duke rolled his eyes around and looked pretty serious. "Yas, sir, I heah," he said.

"An' me an' you, we done made dis bargain on de Lord's birfday—yer heah, boy?—wid Gord's sunshine kiverin' us all over, an' my han' layin' on de page. Heah, lay yo' little han' on top o' mine, Juke, an' promise me you gwine be a *square man*, so he'p yer. Dat's it. Say it out loud, an' yo' ole gran'dad he done said it, too. Wrop up dem fishin'-lines now, an' th'ow 'em up on de rafters. Now come set down heah, an' lemme tell yer 'bout Christmas on de ole plantation. Look out how you pop dat whup 'crost my laig! Dat's a reg'lar horse-fly killer, wid a coal of fire on 'er tip." Duke laughed.

"Now han' me a live coal fur my pipe. Dis here terbacca you brung me, hit smokes sweet as sugar, boy. Set down, now, close by me—so."

Duke never tired of his grandfather's reminiscences, and he crept up close to the old man's knee as the story began.

"When de big plantation-bell used ter ring on Christmas mornin', all de darkies had to march up ter de great house fur dey Christmas-gif's; an' us what worked *at* de house, we had ter stan' in front o' de fiel' han's. An' after ole marster axed a blessin', an' de string-ban' play, an' we all sing a song—air one we choose—boss, he'd call out de names, an' we'd step up, one by one, ter git our presents; an' ef we'd walk too shamefaced ur too 'boveish, he'd pass a joke on us, ter set ev'ybody laughin'.

"I ricollec' one Christmas-time I was co'tin' yo' gran'ma. I done had been co'tin' 'er two years, an' she helt 'er head so high I was 'feerd ter speak. An' when Christmas come, an' I marched up ter git my present, ole marster gimme my bundle, an' I started back, grinnin' lak a chessy-cat, an' he calt me back, an' he say: 'Hol' on, Moses,' he say, 'I got 'nother present fur you ter-day. Heah's a finger-ring I got fur you, an' ef it don't fit you, I reckon hit'll fit Zephyr—you know yo' gran'ma she was name Zephyr. An' wid dat he ran his thumb in 'is pocket an' fotch me out a little gal's ring—"

"A gol' ring, gran'dad?"

"No, boy, but a silver ring—ginniwine German silver. Well, I wush't you could o' heard them darkies holler an' laugh! An' Zephyr, ef she hadn't o' been so yaller, she'd o' been red as dat sky yonder, de way she did blush buff."

"An' what did you do, gran'dad?"

"Who, me? Dey warn't but des one thing *fur* me to do. I des gi'n Zephyr de ring, an' she ax me is I mean it, an'—an' I ax her is *she* mean it, an'—an' we bofe say—none o' yo' business what we say! What you lookin' at me so quizzical fur,

Juke? Ef yer wants ter know, we des had a weddin' dat Christmas night—dat what we done—an' dat's huccome you got yo' gran'ma.

"But I'm talkin' 'bout Christmas now. When we'd all go home, we'd open our bundles, an' of all de purty things, *an'* funny things, *an'* jokes you ever heerd of, dey'd be in dem Christmas bundles—some'h'n' ter suit ev'y one, and hit 'im square on his funny-bone ev'y time. An' all de little bundles o' buckwheat ur flour 'd have *picayunes* an' dimes in 'em! We used ter reg'lar sif' 'em out wid a sifter. Dat was des *our* white folks's way. None o' de yether fam'lies 'long de coas' done it. You see, all de diffe'nt fam'lies had diffe'nt ways. But ole marster an' ole miss dey'd think up some new foolishness ev'y year. We nuver knowed what was gwine to be did nex'—on'y one thing. *Dey allus put money in de buckwheat-bag*—an' you know we nuver tas'e no buckwheat 'cep'n' on'y Christmas. Oh, boy, ef we could des meet wid some o' we's white folks ag'in!"

"How is we got los' fom 'em, gran'dad?" So Duke invited a hundredth repetition of the story he knew so well.

"How did we git los' fom we's white folks? Dat's a sad story fur Christmas, Juke, but ef you sesso—

"Hit all happened in one night, time o' de big break in de levee, seven years gone by. We was lookin' fur de bank ter crack crost de river fom us, an' so boss done had tooken all han's over, cep'n us ole folks an' chillen, ter he'p work an' watch de yether side. 'Bout midnight, whiles we was all sleepin', come a roa'in' soun', an' fus' thing we knowed, all in de pitchy darkness, we was floatin' away—nobody cep'n des you an' me an' yo' mammy in de cabin—floatin' an' bumpin' an' rockin,' *an' all de time dark as pitch*. So we kep' on—one minute stiddy, nex' minute *cher-plunk* gins' a tree ur some'h'n' nother—*all in de dark*—an' one minute you'd cry—you was des a weanin' baby den—an' nex' minute I'd heah de bed you an' yo' ma was in bump gins' de wall, an' you'd laugh out loud, an' yo' mammy she'd holler—*all in de dark*. An' so we travelled, up an' down, bunkety-bunk, seem lak a honderd hours; tell treckly a *termenjus* wave come, an' I had sca'cely felt it boomin' onder me when I pitched, an' ev'ything went travellin'. An' when I put out my han', I felt you by me—but yo' mammy, she warn't nowhar.

"Hol' up yo' face an' don't cry, boy. I been a mighty poor mammy ter yer, but I blesses Gord to-night fur savin' dat little black baby ter me—*all in de win' an' de storm an' de dark dat night.*

"You see, yo' daddy, he was out wid de gang wuckin' de levee crost de river—an' dat's huccome yo' ma was 'feerd ter stay by 'erse'f an' sont fur me.

"Well, baby, when I knowed yo' mammy was gone, I helt you tight an' prayed. An' after a while—seem lak a million hours—come a pale streak o' day, an' 'fo' de sun was up, heah come a steamboat puffin' down de river, an' treckly hit blowed a whistle an' ringed a bell an' stop an' took us on boa'd, an' brung us on down heah ter de city."

"An' you never seed my mammy no mo', gran'dad?" Little Duke's lips quivered just a little.

"Yo' mammy was safe at Home in de Golden City, Juke, long 'fore we teched even de low lan' o' dis yearth.

"An' dat's how we got los' f'om we's white folks.

"An' time we struck de city I was so twis' up wid rheumatiz I lay fur six munts in de Cha'ity Hospit'l; an' you bein' so puny, cuttin' yo' toofs, dey kep' you right along in de baby-ward tell I was able to start out. An' sence I stepped out o' dat hospit'l do' wid yo' little bow-legs trottin' by me, so I been goin' ever sence. Days I'd go out sawin' wood, I'd set you on de wood-pile by me; an' when de cook 'd slip me out a plate o' soup, I'd ax fur two spoons. An' so you an' me, we been pardners right along, an' *I wouldn't swap pardners wid nobody*—you heah, Juke? Dis here's Christmas, an' I'm talkin' ter yer."

Duke looked so serious that a feather's weight would have tipped the balance and made him cry; but he only blinked.

"An' it's gittin' late now, pardner," the old man continued, "an' you better be gwine—less'n you 'feerd? Ef you is, des sesso now, an' we'll meck out wid de col' victuals in de press."

"Who's afeerd, gran'dad?" Duke's face had broken into a broad grin now, and he was cracking his whip again.

"Don't eat no supper tell I come," he added, as he started out into the night. But as he turned down the street he muttered to himself:

"I wouldn't keer, ef all dem sassy boys didn't pleg me—say I ain't got no mammy—ur daddy—ur nothin'. But dey won't say it ter me ag'in, not whiles I got dis whup in my han'! She sting lak a rattlesnake, she do! She's a daisy an' a half! Cher-whack! You gwine sass me any mo', you grea' big over-my-size coward, you? Take dat! An' dat! *An' dat!* Now run! Whoop! Heah come de red light!"

So, in fancy avenging his little wrongs, Duke recovered his spirits and proceeded to catch on behind the Prytania car, that was to help him on his way to get his second-hand Christmas dinner.

His benefactress had not forgotten her promise; and, in addition to a heavy pan of scraps, Duke took home, almost staggering beneath its weight, a huge, compact bundle.

Old Mose was snoring vociferously when he reached the cabin. Depositing his parcel, the little fellow lit a candle, which he placed beside the sleeper; then uncovering the pan, he laid it gently upon his lap. And now, seizing a spoon and tin cup, he banged it with all his might.

"Heah de plantation-bell! Come git yo' Christmas-gif's!"

And when his grandfather sprang up, nearly upsetting the pan in his fright, Duke rolled backward on the floor, screaming with laughter.

"I 'clare, Juke, boy," said Mose, when he found voice, "I wouldn't 'a' jumped so, but yo' foolishness des fitted inter my dream. I was dreamin' o' ole times, an' des when I come ter de ringin' o' de plantation-bell, I heerd *cherplang*! An' it nachelly riz me off'n my foots. What's dis heah? Did you git de dinner, sho' 'nough?"

The pan of scraps quite equalled that of the old man's memory, every familiar fragment evoking a reminiscence.

"You is sho' struck quality white folks dis time, Juke," he said, finally, as he pushed back the pan—Duke had long ago finished—"but dis here tukkey-stuffin'—I don't say 'tain' good, but *hit don't quite come up ter de mark o' ole miss's puckon stuffin'!*"

Duke was nodding in his chair, when presently the old man, turning to go to bed, spied the unopened parcel, which, in his excitement, Duke had forgotten. Placing it upon the table before him, Mose began to open it. It was a package worth getting—just such a generous Christmas bundle as he had described to Duke this afternoon. Perhaps it was some vague impression of this sort that made his old fingers tremble as he untied the strings, peeping or sniffing into the little parcels of tea and coffee and flour. Suddenly something happened. Out of a little sack of buckwheat, accidentally upset, rolled a ten-cent piece. The old man threw up his arms, fell forward over the table, and in a moment was sobbing aloud.

It was some time before he could make Duke comprehend the situation, but presently, pointing to the coin lying before him, he cried: "Look, boy, look! Wharbouts is you got dat bundle? Open yo' mouf, boy! Look at de money in de buckwheat-bag! Oh, my ole mistuss! Nobody but you is tied up dat bundle! Praise Gord, I say!"

There was no sleep for either Mose or Duke now; and, late as it was, they soon started out, the old man steadying himself on Duke's shoulder, to find their people.

It was hard for the little boy to believe, even after they had hugged all 'round and laughed and cried, that the stylish black gentleman who answered the door-bell, silver tray in hand, was his own father! He had often longed for a regular blue-shirted plantation "daddy," but never, in his most ambitious moments, had he aspired to filial relations with so august a personage as this!

But while Duke was swelling up, rolling his eyes, and wondering, Mose stood in the centre of a crowd of his white people, while a gray-haired old lady, holding his trembling hand in both of hers, was saying, as the tears trickled down her cheeks:

"But why didn't you get some one to write to us for you, Moses?"

Then Mose, sniffling still, told of his long illness in the hospital, and of his having afterwards met a man from the coast who told the story of the sale of the plantation, but did not know where the family had gone.

"When I fixed up that bundle," the old lady resumed, "I was thinking of you, Moses. Every year we have sent out such little packages to any needy colored people of whom we knew, as a sort of memorial to our lost ones, always half-hoping that they might actually reach some of them. And I thought of you specially, Moses," she continued, mischievously, "when I put in all that turkey-stuffing. Do you remember how greedy you always were about pecan-stuffing? It wasn't quite as good as usual this year."

"No'm; dat what I say," said Mose. "I tol' Juke dat stuffin' warn't quite up ter de mark—ain't I, Juke? Fur gracious sake, look at Juke, settin' on his daddy's shoulder, with a face on him ole as a man! Put dat boy down, Pete! Dat's a business-man you foolin' wid!"

Whereupon little Duke—man of affairs, forager, financier—overcome at last with the fulness of the situation, made a really babyish square mouth, and threw himself sobbing upon his father's bosom.

FOOTNOTE:

Pronounced lan-yap. *Lagniappe* is a small gratuity which New Orleans children always expect and usually get with a purchase. Retail druggists keep jars of candy, licorice, or other small confections for that purpose.

UNCLE EPHE'S ADVICE TO BRER RABBIT

"'KEEP STEP, RABBIT, MAN!'"

UNCLE EPHE'S ADVICE TO BRER RABBIT

Keep step, Rabbit, man! Hunter comin' quick's he can! H'ist yo'se'f! *Don't* cross de road, Less 'n he'll hit you fur a toad!

Up an' skip it, 'fo' t's too late! Hoppit—lippit! Bull-frog gait! Hoppit—lippit—lippit—hoppit! Goodness me, why don't you stop it?

Shame on you, Mr. Ge'man Rabbit, Ter limp along wid sech a habit! 'F you'd balumps on yo' hime-legs straight, An' hurry wid a mannish gait,

An' tie yo' ears down onder yo' th'oat, An' kivir yo' tail wid a cut-away coat, Rabbit-hunters by de dozen Would shek yo' han' an' call you cousin,

An' like as not, you onery sinner, Dey'd ax' you home ter eat yo' dinner! But *don't you go*, 'caze ef you do, Dey'll set you down to rabbit-stew.

An' de shape o' dem bones an' de smell o' dat meal 'Ll meck you wish you was back in de fiel'. An' ef you'd stretch yo' mouf too wide, You know yo' ears mought come ontied;

An' when you'd jump, you couldn't fail To show yo' little cotton tail, An' den, 'fo' you could twis' yo' phiz, Dey'd *reconnize* you *who you is*;

An' fo' you'd sca'cely bat yo' eye, Dey'd have you skun an' in a pie, Or maybe roasted on a coal, Widout one thought about yo' soul.

So better teck ole Ephe's advice, Des rig yo'se'f out slick an' nice, An' tie yo' ears down, like I said, An' hide yo' tail an' lif' yo' head.

"'WELL, ONE MO' RABBIT FUR DE POT'"

An' when you balumps on yo' foots, It wouldn't hurt ter put on boots. Den walk *straight up*, like Mr. Man, An' when he offer you 'is han',

Des smile, an' gi'e yo' hat a tip; But *don't you show yo' rabbit lip*. An' don't you have a word ter say, No mo'n ter pass de time o' day.

An' ef he ax 'bout yo' affairs, Des 'low you gwine ter hunt some hares, An' ax 'im is he seen a jack— An' dat 'll put 'im off de track.

Now, ef you'll foller dis advice, Instid o' bein' et wid rice, Ur baked in pie, ur stuffed wid sage, You'll live ter die of nachel age.

'Sh! hush! What's dat? Was dat a gun? *Don't* trimble so. An' *don't you run*! Come, set heah on de lorg wid me— Hol' down yo' ears an' cross yo' knee.

Don't run, *I say*. Tut—tut! He's gorn. *Right 'cross de road*, as sho's you born! Slam bang! I know'd he'd ketch a shot! Well, one mo' rabbit fur de pot!

MAY BE SO

MAY BE SO

September butterflies flew thick O'er flower-bed and clover-rick, When little Miss Penelope, Who watched them from grandfather's knee,

Said, "Grandpa, what's a butterfly?" And, "Where do flowers go to when they die?" For questions hard as hard can be I recommend Penelope.

But grandpa had a playful way Of dodging things too hard to say, By giving fantasies instead Of serious answers, so he said,

"Whenever a tired old flower must die, Its soul mounts in a butterfly; Just now a dozen snow-wings sped From out that white petunia bed;

"And if you'll search, you'll find, I'm sure, A dozen shrivelled cups or more; Each pansy folds her purple cloth, And soars aloft in velvet moth.

"So when tired sunflower doffs her cap Of yellow frills to take a nap, 'Tis but that this surrender brings Her soul's release on golden wings."

"But *is this so*? It ought to be," Said little Miss Penelope; "Because I'm *sure*, dear grandpa, *you* Would only tell the thing that's *true*.

"Are all the butterflies that fly Real angels of the flowers that die?" Grandfather's eyes looked far away, As if he scarce knew what to say.

"Dear little Blossom," stroking now The golden hair upon her brow, "I can't—exactly—say—I—know—it; I only heard it from a poet.

"And poets' eyes see wondrous things. Great mysteries of flowers and wings, And marvels of the earth and sea And sky, they tell us constantly.

"But we can never prove them right, Because we lack their finer sight; And they, lest we should think them wrong, Weave their strange stories into song

"*So beautiful*, so *seeming-true*, So confidently stated too, That we, not knowing yes or no, Can only *hope they may be so*."

"But, grandpapa, no tale should close With *ifs* or *buts* or *may-be-sos*; So let us play we're poets, too, And then we'll *know* that this is true."

THE END

CPSIA information can be obtained at www.ICGtesting.com
Printed in the USA
BVOW04s1721080415

395328BV00013B/167/P